I0666390

STRUGGLE

First Edition

Published by The Nazca Plains Corporation
Las Vegas, Nevada
2008

ISBN: 978-1-934625-73-6

Published by

The Nazca Plains Corporation ®
4640 Paradise Rd, Suite 141
Las Vegas NV 89109-8000

PUBLISHER'S NOTE
Struggle is a work of fiction created wholly by *Christopher Trevor's* imagination. All characters are fictional and any resemblance to any persons living or deceased is purely by accident. No portion of this book reflects any real person or events.

Cover, Joao
Art Director, Blake Stephens

DEDICATION

To my good friend, Rich,
AKA catinhat@myfriendsfeet...

Struggle

First Edition

Christopher Trevor

CONTENTS

INTRODUCTION FOR

"STRUGGLE"

Written by: Timmy Backman (with one hand tied behind him) and embellished by: Christopher Trevor

Ah, the joys of bondage and struggling. Where shall I begin? First and foremost, when entering into games involving bondage please be sure to know and trust the person you are allowing to tie you, chain you, blindfold you, gag you, etc. While bondage can be great fun and struggling against it even more thrilling one must always be cautious in this arena as well. As for me, Timmy Backman, ever gullible bondage and tickle hero/victim (as I have come to be known as) I should know about these things. You see, since meeting the author Christopher Trevor I have spent an inordinate amount of time in bondage and struggling. Seems my good buddy just loves tying me...and I just love a good struggle...

WHOA! Tied up again, this time with one hand behind me as

I am forced to type this introduction for Christopher Trevor's latest book. The only way to enjoy bondage and struggling against the forces that hold you is to struggle even harder against even more diabolical bondage, bondage that screams control. But, in the joy of it, it is control that I have lost, control that resides in someone else. I get to live out my bondage fantasies under the ever watchful control of my mentor/tormentor, Christopher Trevor. The man has a devilish imagination and I am continually subjected to those devilish, dominant schemes. Oh, if I had a nickel for every bondage and tickle fantasy Christopher has subjected me to. Under his gaze and control the root of my being springs to life as I feel the tightening confines of my bondage. Christopher's belief is that my root tells the truth of how much I love being knotted up in ropes and made to struggle. I can protest all I want he says, but an erect cock does not lie. And the more I struggle the more helpless I feel, and the more helpless I feel, the more I struggle and the more I struggle the more my root grows. It is a vicious cycle of helpless sexy struggle and the exhilaration of the total loss of control. It is that loss of control and the struggles against that which binds me is amazingly stimulating somehow. Most times my tormentor Christopher Trevor ties and blindfolds me, making it all the more difficult for me to even try to work myself free. The only thing that turns my attention away from that sexual stew is the teasing; tickling torments that Christopher puts me through while I struggle against my bonds. It's wonderful yet maddening at the same time. AWWWWW and it looks like this time, like other times he has tied the knots so that when I struggle the knots tend to get tighter. How does he do that???

And now in Mr. Trevor's latest book we will read of other guy's besides me and their bondage struggles. The book opens with a tale of edging and bondage as I once again submit to my mentor/tormentor. Once more I have agreed to a contest of strength and endurance at the hands and ropes of Christopher Trevor. Oh my word, this time I just might win and turn the tables on that diabolical author. In the story "Chuck's Ticklish Plight", a groom to be is abducted along with his bride to be by unknown ski masked assailants. Daisy sits tied to a chair and watches and listens as her hunky groom to be is tickled past the points of endurance. In keeping with the title of this book, the groom struggles superbly. The book is rounded out by the tale that inspired the title, a harrowing story of struggle and bondage and fiendish games...inspired by a video that the author viewed and turned into an erotic tale of abduction, fetishism and struggles...

Happy Reading,

Timmy Backman

FANTASY

The Beginning

"How long has it been since you've cum? How long since you shot your load my handsome laddy?" Christopher asked me, sounding totally mocking as he drank in and devoured the sight of me, the sight of how he had me securely tethered at the moment.

We both knew very well how long it had been since I had cum, how very long it had been since I had shot my load. He knew and I knew but part of the author's loving sadism was making me recite my plight, my goddamned quandary, him listening to me tell of my torments got his nut somehow.

"Ninety nine days," I responded thickly and gutturally, straining against the bonds holding my muscular arms to the headboard.

My word, why had I allowed the author to tie me up this way? Because he loves me in bondage that's why. And I can't resist him that's why. And because I'm just a horned up guy who just can't say no it seems... Naked but for those black nylon socks he loves me in, OTCs to be exact, and tied in a spread eagle position of all things, all my sexy parts available for his pleasures...and it was one area in particular that he planned to work for the moment, oh my word of words...what had I gotten myself into this time?

The author knelt between my stretched out muscular legs, my black socked ankles tied off at the bed's legs. My socks had ribbed and scrunched up a bit in some sections, that's how long I had been tied and squirming at that point. But all of that combined just made the author love me all the more it seemed. Having me tied was his way of showing me how much I mean to him, how much he cares for me, twisted yes, but exciting at the same time. Don't ask me to explain it; it's the dynamics of our relationship. He had the lube glistening on his fingers in the candlelight of the hotel room we were in. With a wicked looking smile on his face he worked the lube into my most private crevice, namely my asshole, speaking to me in a loving manner the whole time, as if what he was doing to me was perfectly status quo, what two buddies always do to each other, one ties the other up and torments him, HA!

"Ninety nine days and twenty three hours," Christopher said, all the while two of his lubed up fingers were prodding around in my shit chute, moistening me up back there. The sounds of squishing were maddening as he played my hole like it was an instrument. And straight as I am I was responding to it, OH MY WORD!

"Almost done aren't we?" Christopher asked me teasingly. "Tomorrow, or should I say in one more hour it will be one hundred days. I can just imagine, being a guy as well, how those balls of yours must be feeling. You must be very, very excited by now."

I squirmed on the bed, curled my toes under my socks and

he teased my rock hard cock and churning balls until I groaned an agreement.

"And I promised you Timmy, that if you adhered to the rules of the game I put forth for you and that if you could hold out for one hundred days, then I would allow you to have your tickle ways with me for a change...right?" the author asked me and snaked his fingers back into my oven of an asshole.

I groaned anew as his fingers prodded me back there...

"Yes, you being tied up, you being tickled to death and screaming with laughter for a change Mr. Author," I garbled and gasped as his fingers did their work in my hole. "For a whole month... *for a whole month* I would get to tickle torment you, the tables turned in my favor for a change. Oh yes, what an exquisite picture that is to behold..."

As I spoke Christopher looked at me with adoration, I knew how much he loved my Southern accent, what he called my "Senator John Edwards" Southern accent.

"And yes, yes," I whispered huskily. "Just another hour or so to go..."

It was a good game, but with a terrible penalty. It seemed that Christopher loved balancing me on these narrow ledges he called predicaments. And my word and woe is me but I always agreed to his games. My submissive nature and Christopher Trevor's wicked imagination was a match made in some twisted heaven, or hell, depending on how you looked at it. A good game, with a terrible penalty, in that, if I came without permission then I would have to start over for another hundred days and not cum again, woe is me. And if I did cum before the time was up I would also have to wait to tickle tease my constant tormentor as well... Paradoxically, it did get easier as time went on. I was somehow able to allow my focus on my body to go elsewhere. Well, most of the time anyway, but during the last few days I'd been feeling my composure slipping as the deadline started to near. There were just so many cold showers I could take and so much working out at the gym that I could go to allay my desires. And not having sex with the wife, well, that was a chore in and of itself let me tell you. Thank heavens I had business trips to go on and such. But at the moment I had the bluest case of blue balls ever known to man.

"Now, do you know what this is?" Christopher asked and held up a black rubbery device, showing it to me as he poured some of the lube over it.

I knew what it was and I was between a rock and a hard place in knowing what the author was going to do with it. He hadn't been slopping his lubed fingers around in my asshole for nothing after all.

"It's a butt-plug," he went on. "I read in one of your Timmy Backman tickle stories that it was something you wanted to try, something you were...curious about my handsome laddy?"

I sucked in my breath as he smiled and eased the plug into my lubed and sopped ass.

"Oh my word, oh my fucks," I moaned through clenched teeth as the thing slid slowly and slimy inside me.

"I ordered it a couple of weeks ago," Christopher said as he stretched me with the thing. "It's quite the toy my boy."

As Christopher slid the thing in some more it stretched my crevice walls, and then the sudden clenching as my muscles back there clamped onto the smaller diameter. I closed my eyes, panting slightly.

"And do you know what this is?" he asked again.

I opened my eyes to see that my male tormentor was holding

up a rubber squeeze bulb.

"You see, it's an inflatable butt-plug that I inserted into you," Christopher said mockingly. "Good thing I tied you up yes Timmy?"

As I opened my mouth to answer, to plead maybe, he gave the thing a squeeze and said, "One."

I gritted my jaw as the thing in my ass seemed to swell. He paused for ten seconds or so, watching me carefully, adoring the sight of me tied up in just those OTC black nylon socks.

"Two," he counted, giving the bulb another squeeze.

Again I felt the plug inflate.

Another ten second pause and Christopher said, "Three."

This time the expansion in my hole made me twitch.

"Four," Christopher laughed.

I started clenching my muscles, knowing that the plug was expanding deeper inside me, tormenting me erotically.

"Five," Christopher whispered and squeezed the bulb.

By now I could really feel the plug stretching my insides. I rocked my hips on the bed, but that only served to make it stimulate me.

"Six," the author said and squeezed the bulb with one hand, his other hand caressing my chock filled nuts.

Involuntarily I let out a whimper.

"Oh, do you like that?" Christopher asked me. "It must feel

really nice, being all full. I'm sure its pressing up against your prostate by now. Is your head spinning Timmy?"

I nodded. Every movement seemed to excite me now and I could feel my composure slipping. Somehow Christopher was controlling me with that danged butt-plug that was wedged inside me.

"Seven," Christopher said, sounding sexy as all hell.

He squeezed the bulb and I let out a small moan.

"Yeah, nudging up against your prostate, all swollen from not coming for ninety nine days," Christopher teased me. "Look, your cock is all swollen too. It must be getting hard to hold back, huh?"

I shook my head back and forth. My cock had become a skyscraper between my stretched out and tied legs. I was hard as steel...

"No, no, I'm fine," I lied as I wondered why in the hell I had agreed to this exquisite torture.

My voice sounded high and weak...

"Sure you are," he replied and held up the bulb. "Eight..."

I could feel my arms trembling. My feet were sweating in those danged black socks the author insisted I wear. I had arrived there in blue jeans, a white pullover Polo shirt, a black leather jacket, dock shoes, and danged black socks. Always, my socks had to be black and nylon for the author. Most times I wear either good old white sweat socks with my dock shoes or maybe beige, but for Christopher my socks had to be black nylon. My word, besides the way my feet looked all sexy and vulnerable in those black socks the author loved the scent they gave off...just like they were doing now as I sweated in them. I tried to breathe through my mouth, slow, measured breaths until I heard...

"Nine," Christopher said.

I bit down hard on my lip. I thought about all the times Christopher had tormented me tickle wise and this was the price I was paying to finally have my revenge. The thing was filling me, both painful and pleasurable. Each motion nudged me just a teeny bit closer to losing control.

"Oh Timmy, my handsome Timmy, wouldn't it be a real bitch if you shot your load now, with only less than an hour to go?" Christopher asked me, massaging my balls as he spoke. "All that time, only to have to start over again?"

As I looked up at him desperately from my tied up position he smirked at me. I tried not to move. When I looked down I saw the clear fluid seeping from my erect and engorged cock. It was dripping onto my stomach. Christopher followed my gaze and arched an eyebrow. He reached down and gave a slow stroke to my lengthy erection. I tried to move my hips away, only to make the plug nudge my sensitive spot deep inside. Oh no, I thought. I was starting to feel some involuntary contractions.

"Ten," Christopher laughed and I let out a long moan and writhed on the bed.

"No, no, no, no!" I begged. "That's not fair!"

"Would you like for me to stop pumping?" Christopher asked.

I nodded.

"Yes, please, please, please, no more, I can't take anymore, it's gonna split me open!" I babbled.

Every time I clenched my muscles to hold back the plug nudged me a little more. I was on the edge of cumming, of exploding and maddeningly without even touching my swollen and tortured cock.

"I think that I'm going to leave you like this for a while Timmy," Christopher stated, starting to climb off the bed.

I looked at him, pleading in my eyes.

"But don't worry, I'm not going to pump you anymore, okay?" he asked me, trying to sound as reassuring as possible.

I nodded, relaxing my tense and tied body just a bit...

"Because it would be a real shame if you shot your load now, with only..." he looked at the clock. "...with only fifty minutes or so to go, wouldn't it?"

"Y-yes Christopher," I whispered. "Thank you..."

I closed my eyes and tried to focus through the delirium of sexual desire that was consuming me. Breathe in; hold, yes, that's it. Yes, that's it, breathe out. The contractions stopped. Breathe in, hold. I was winning. Breathe out. I was regaining my control. Breathe in...

"Do you know what this is?" I heard Christopher ask me as he stood by the foot of the bed, rubbing one of his legs against one of my bound up socked feet.

I opened my eyes and nearly gasped. He was holding an electronic control in his hand.

"Did I mention that it's a *vibrating*, inflatable butt-plug?" he asked with a look of buddy sweetness. "And Timmy, I just put in fresh batteries. Lets see if they'll last an hour..."

He pressed a button on the electronic gizmo and I pursed my lips tightly...

"Oh my word..." was all I could say...

FANTASY

Part 1

"Oh my word," I said again, gasping this time as Christopher pressed a button on the electronic control for the inflated butt-plug that he had wedged into my hole not minutes ago.

I was feeling all stopped up in my shit chute yet totally aroused and excited as that danged device filled me back there. I squirmed on the bed I was tied to in a spread-eagle position, my black socked heels rubbing against the sheets I lay on. As Christopher pressed the button on the electronic control in his hand I waited for the buzzing sensations to begin in my most private crevice. He had teasingly told me that besides the thing inside my rectal hole being an inflatable butt-plug, that it was also a vibrating one as well, oh woe is me. And if that thing started buzzing like a swarm of bees in my hole I would be literally cooked back there. I would also more than likely shoot my danged load without even having my cock touched, that was how horned up and sensitized I was at the moment. Ah hell, you try not shooting your load for one hundred days and see if the slightest touch or twinge doesn't make you cum, hell! Christopher smiled wickedly at me as he held the button down on the electronic control. But when no buzzing sound was heard and no buzzing sensations were felt by me in my hole we both looked perplexed, for obviously different reasons. I glanced at my sides at my bound up wrists tethered to the bed board and then looked straight ahead at the man who had so lovingly put me in this position, at the man that *I had allowed* to put me in this position. Believe you me buds, I don't just let any guy tie me the fuck up, that's for sure...although over time I have been tricked and cajoled into being tied up by a number of crafty guys, hardy har, har for me I suppose...

"Something wrong bud?" I asked the author. "I thought you said you just put fresh batteries in that thing-um-a-jig..."

"I did," Christopher said a worried look on his handsome face.

He glanced at me, glanced at the electronic gizmo in his hand and then glanced at the clock.

"Forty five minutes to go," I chuckled and squirmed in my tight rope bondage. "And if you don't make me cum in that time I win this sadistic little game of yours and the tables turn...and you know what that means Mr. Author Sir."

As I lay there feeling a sense of satisfaction Christopher clenched his teeth and pressed the button again on the electronic device in his hand.

"*Shit, shit,*" he whispered and looked down at me, desperation now showing in his eyes. "I should just suck you off, we both know how much you love when I do that to you, I'll even blindfold you for it so you can pretend its Valerie doing you..."

"Oh yes, that would be heaven in my cock, but it would also be cheating Christopher," I said with a grin. "Remember the rules of this game you put forth when you presented it to me some time ago. You have to get me off without touching my cock. You have to make me shoot my load involuntarily."

Christopher dropped the electronic control on the bed between my legs and huffed a few times...

"Feeling a tad nervous buddy?" I asked him, wiggling my toes in my sweaty and moist black OTC socks. "Just think, in another forty five minutes our roles here will be reversed."

"It ain't over till its over," Christopher said meanly.

As Christopher stood there looking at me hungrily and desperately, (I knew from past experience how much he loved chowing and sucking on my manhood, and this time he couldn't do that, at least not yet) I thought back to how this most recent contest between us had begun. As usual it was Christopher's idea to make me the victim in this sadistically amusing predicament. We had been internet chatting about new ideas for new tickle tales starring yours truly, Timmy Backman as the ever-constant tickle victim/hero. The chat had somehow moved on to edging and keeping a guy constantly horned up by not letting himself cum for a lengthy period of time.

"How long do you think you could keep yourself from cumming my laddy?" Christopher asked me.

Sitting there at my computer, safe in my home I laughed at his question and rubbed my ever hard cock through my khaki pants. Somehow I knew that Christopher had a predicament in mind for me yet again...and being that he had called me "laddy" I knew I would agree to what was churning in that imagination of his.

"I would reckon a few days I could hold out," I replied and Christopher replied by saying "LOL" (laughing out loud) and <Evil Grin>

Somehow I knew I had stepped into it again...

"One hundred days my laddy," Christopher typed and my heart thudded in mortal fear.

One hundred days? One hundred days for a guy not to shoot his load? But as apprehensive as I was feeling I agreed to it. I asked my loving tormentor the rules...

Christopher said that I was not to cum, not under any circumstances for one hundred days, starting from the moment we signed off the computers. I asked him how he knew I would stick to my end of the deal. We don't live nearby each other so that he could keep tabs on me after all. He said that he trusted me and knew that I was a man of my word. Dang, why was I born so honest and forthright? I then asked him what would happen at the end of the hundred days. Christopher laughingly told me that my balls would be swollen to the size of inflatable balloons. Seriously, he said that we would meet in a hotel room where he would make me shoot my load involuntarily, maybe. I told him he would not be able to get me off, no matter what he did. At that Christopher said he loved a challenge. He went on to say that he had ways of getting me off, even without having to touch my manhood. Sitting there now with a rage hard-on I typed "LOL" and Christopher said that the only two things I would have to agree to for the game would be to allow him to tie me up when the time came for us to meet and for me to wear his favorites, the black nylon socks. Now Christopher had tied me up in the past so I was fine with allowing that, I always wore black socks for him so I was fine with that too. But as for not shooting my load for one hundred days, well, that was not going to be easy. I'm a married guy after all. My wife Stephanie is sexy as all hell and then there's the sexually wicked and evil Valerie. Hell, Valerie is a story in and of herself. Christopher said that if I did cum between the moment we were chatting and the time we met I was to tell him, and the contest would start anew, with me having to not shoot my load for the next hundred days. I then set forth my end of the deal, that if I did not shoot my load for a hundred days and that if when we met my author buddy did not get me off then he would have to become my tickle slave for a change. I saw that there were a few moments of hesitation before Christopher typed me a reply. Then, when he did reply he said that he agreed to my terms as well, but he knew that he would win the game when we met...

My mind and thoughts were suddenly and abruptly brought back to the present as I was now uncontrollably laughing my fool head off...

"HAR, HAR, HAR!" was the sound filling the hotel room I was tied to the bed in as I laughed like a loon.

After his electronic control device didn't work to start the butt-plug buzzing in my hole Christopher had resorted to tickling my danged black socked feet. Well, resorted really isn't the word I'm looking for here. Once I was stripped down and tied up I knew the author would tickle my danged socked feet, it wouldn't be a contest for us if he didn't. To be more precise here Christopher was lick-tickling my black socked feet...alternately. We had thirty-five minutes to go...I had to hold out for that length of time buds...I had to laugh and hold out... oh woe is me...

At the side of the bed where my left socked foot was tethered at the ankle Christopher was kneeling comfortably. He was holding my foot straight up by a handful of my toes and my arch as he slid and slithered the tip of his pointy tongue up and down the meaty bottom of it.

"YAAAAAAAA, ha, ha, ha!" I screamed and my stiff and rigid cock bucked and twitched between my muscular spread out legs. "Oh dang it all Christopher, this isn't fair...y-you're ticklin' my feet is goin' to make me cum after all...HAHAHA!"

"Precisely my laddy, and we all know how tickling really gets Timmy Backman off," Christopher laughed, held tight to my arch area, kissed the bottom of my socked foot a few times and then wriggled his fingertips over and over my danged toes, tickling them now.

"Ha, ha, ha!" I laughed crazily. "I'll hold out, you'll see, I won't cum, I WILL NOT CUM FOR YOU! HAHAHA!"

Then, I watched through tear soaked laughter filled eyes as my buddy tickled my toes and the bottom of my socked foot, his hands moving at almost bionic-like speed it seemed.

"OHHHHHHHHH, HAR, HAR, HAR!" I crowed loudly, my tied hands clenched into fists at my sides.

I looked up at the clock and wondered if I would be able to hold out for another thirty to thirty-five minutes. My hard cock waved in the air and dribbled large dollops of pre-seed. It was so danged sexy to see my pre-seed seeping from my slit and onto my stomach area. No, no, I could not cum, I had to finally win one here...

As I laughed crazily as my good buddy lick tickled my danged tied up feet I steered my mind back again to my arrival at the hotel where Christopher now had me...

I had arrived promptly at the appointed time, two hours before I was to cum to be exact. Christopher, being the anal guy he is when it comes to time had planned this perfectly to the minute. He had rented a hotel room for us in a ritzy and fashionable hotel in the heart of New York City's Time Square area, nice and fancy and soundproof. The fact that the room was soundproof told me I would be laughing while being tickled at some point, and laughing pretty loudly at that I figured...

I walked up to the front desk of the hotel at ten minutes before the time I was to be in the room with my tormentor. I had just one small piece of luggage for this trip, which contained only a change of clothes for my trip home and men's toiletries. I told the desk clerk that I was there to meet Christopher Trevor and asked what room he was in. The gay desk clerk looked at my a tad hungrily and jealously and then directed me to the elevators after telling me that Christopher Trevor was in room 1018. It seemed that room number was the one my buddy always occupied when in hotels. I had to wonder if it was a lucky number for him or something like that. I rode the elevator to the tenth floor, shucking off my leather jacket as I ascended. When I got to the room I knocked softly and Christopher opened the door a few seconds later. At the sight of me his eyes lit up. He was dressed pretty much like me in jeans and a pullover shirt.

"Man, it seems that no matter how often we get together for these romps of ours you never fail to take my breath away my handsome laddy," Christopher said as I grinned and stepped into the room.

He closed the door behind me as I chucked my leather jacket onto a sofa. Looking at each other we hugged tightly then, holding tight to each other.

"Oh Timmy, it's always so good to see you," Christopher said and I could hear the tears in his voice as he choked.

He held me tighter, one hand smoothing the hair on the back of my head and then squeezing the back of my neck. I didn't stop him as he pressed his lips against my neck and pecked me gently a few times.

"It's always good to see you too buddy," I whispered as the man held me.

He rubbed his crotch against mine and whispered in my ear, "It feels like Ringling Brothers has pitched a hard tent in your jeans my laddy." I grinned as the author again smoothed the hair on the back of my head (he seemed to love doing that) and replied, "Well, you hold out from cumming for one hundred days and see if your cock doesn't inflate a bit." At that we both laughed and Christopher held me tighter and again kissed the side of my neck. I knew that just the sound of my Southern accent was enough to get him in motion.

Dang, I wasn't the only one who had a tent pitched in his pants at that moment. My author buddy was pretty erect and stacked up as well in the area of his manhood.

"Besides your cock being inflated a bit how are your balls feeling?" Christopher asked me.

I chuckled a bit as we disengaged from each other and then held Christopher by his upper arms as we looked at each other.

"Lets say this where my danged balls are concerned bud, I feel like I have two lead bowling balls in my danged underpants, that's how big and sore they feel," I said and we both laughed.

Then, letting go of Christopher's arms I glanced to my right and saw the bed and the way Christopher had it prepared for me... On each side of the head board I saw that lengths of rope had been wound and that the slack of the rope was strewn across the bed itself. The same held for the foot area of the bed, more rope wound about the legs of the bed and the slack of it strewn at the foot area atop the bed itself.

"Looks like you're all ready for me buddy," I said and Christopher pointed at the clock on the wall.

"Two hours Timmy, two more hours till the game is over," Christopher said and this time he took me by my arm as we approached the bed.

When we were standing next to the bed my heart was pounding in a mixture of fear and excitement. Christopher held tight to my arm and watched as I took in the sight of the ropes...

"Thinking of backing out?" he asked me.

I turned to him, smiled a bit and then stepped out of my dock shoes, revealing my black nylon socked feet.

"I guess not," the author said jovially, sounding sadistic at the same time I shucked off my shirt, revealing my muscular and well toned chest.

"Let the game begin, buddy..." I said, trying to sound as confident as possible.

FANTASY

Part 2

"YAHHHHHH, ha, ha, ha!" I laughed loudly as Christopher was now tickle torturing my right black socked foot.

He had moved from my left foot to my right foot, not giving me much time whatsoever to catch my breath as he switched position. Like with my left foot he began by grabbing me by a handful of my moist socked toes with one hand, his other hand gripping my arch and then he slathered the tip of his tongue up and down the bottom of my foot, lick tickling me.

"Just about ready to cum my laddy?" Christopher teased and quickly resumed flicking his tongue tip over and over the bottom of my danged foot.

"NO, NO, you will not win this one Christopher, HAHAHA!" I replied, clenched my teeth to hold back more laughter but erupted wildly when the author slid a fingertip over the balls of my right foot. "AHHHHHHHHHHHH, ha, ha, ha! J-just another twenty five minutes to go buddy...we'll see how you take to being tied and tickled and tormented...HAHAHA!"

Amazing as it was, even to me, I was winning, I had not shot my load yet, and I had adhered to the rules of this twisted game between two willing guys. Granted, I was hornier than ever before in all my life, the way my pre-seed was dripping so freely from my erection attested to that. But I hadn't done the deed of shooting my real gusher. And if I didn't cum for the next twenty five minutes I would have won this game I had been cajoled into. Dang, one hundred days that I hadn't been allowed to shoot my danged load! How sadistic is that for any guy I ask you. I looked up at the clock through my tear filled laughter eyes and screamed out like a loon...

My mind wandered back again to my arrival at the hotel where Christopher was presently holding me as his tickle and edging slave...

Standing next to the bed after I had slipped my dock shoes and pullover shirt off Christopher asked me again if I was thinking about backing out.

"After not shooting my load for a hundred days do you think I'm going to back out now Mr. Author Sir?" I asked him as I stood there with my muscular chest jutted out, unbuttoning my jeans.

Christopher looked anxiously at the queen-sized bed where at each end of it was rope lashed to the bed board and the bed legs, the slack of the rope waiting to bind me. Looking at the rope and knowing that in moments I would be tied and immobilized in just my danged socks sent a chill of wonderment through me. Woe is me, but I really am a submissive boy.

"Once you're tied to that bed all deals are off my laddy," Christopher said and brazenly twisted and tweaked one of my bubbled up man sized tits.

I moaned in a man's passion at my good buddy's touch and pushed my jeans down around my ankles, revealing the tops of my OTC black nylon socks as they just about kissed my knees and my trademark kangaroo pouch style boxer briefs... The front-most section of my boxer briefs were stained with pre-seed. After only twenty days of not shooting my load I was pre-seeding like a leaky faucet. By now I was pre-seeding every moment of the day it seemed.

I stepped out of my jeans, kicked them aside and it was Christopher who did the honors of de-under-panting me. I stood all sexy and docile as he hooked his fingers around the sides of my under shorts, snapped the elastic in them against my skin a few times and then slid them down my muscular tree-trunk-like legs.

"Oh my word..." I breathed heavily as Christopher hunkered down in front of me, helping me off with my under shorts by grasping first one of my black socked calves to balance me and then the other.

When I was naked but for my socks I watched as my author buddy stole a few sniffs of my sore and overly cum filled balls. My cock was a thing of steel between my legs and pointing straight up at me. Christopher ran the palms of his hands over my socked calves and gave my aching balls a few good licks and slathers. Chills coursed through me and goose bumps broke out all over me as he teased my testicles in an oral fashion...but he didn't touch my cock at all. That was off limits for the next two hours or so. If he were to make me cum it had to be without touching my manhood.

"Your throne my handsome laddy," Christopher said, squeezing my upper arm and gesturing at the bed.

I gulped hard and lay down on my back, spreading my arms and legs out real wide...

A few minutes later I was tied to the bed in a spread eagle position, stretched out real tight in the bondage. Christopher had tied my feet to the bed first, making me watch while my hands were still free. It was a bit unnerving, knowing that with my hands still free I could still stop him and end this game...but I didn't, I *didn't* bud. Watching that guy tie my black socked feet to the bed was intense somehow. My cock throbbed and pulsed harder and stiffer as the guy stole a few sniffs of my socked feet while tying them. Then, I lay back and allowed the guy to bind my wrists to the bed board. When he was done I was his yet again...and the games of torment and to get me to shoot my load had begun in earnest...

"HAHAHA, we now have ten minutes Christopher!" I hawed loudly as the guy was now using the pointy ends of toothpicks to tickle my danged black socked feet with.

By then I was bathed in sweat and writhing wildly on the bed. I was so close to winning this game that I could not believe it. Ten more minutes, that was all I had to endure buds...

With a look of utter desperation in his eyes now Christopher abandoned my feet and started in tickling another sensitive part of me, namely my armpits. He began at my right sided pit, digging his fingers of both hands deep in my hairy bush.

"HARRRRRRRRRRR!" I roared and my handsome mug scrunched up as I exploded into fits of loud and wild laughter.

"Cum my laddy, cum for me," Christopher whispered, he and I both glancing at the clock now.

"OH MY WORD, OH MY FUCKING WORD!" I railed as he straddled me then on the bed and dug his fingers into both of my smelly and sweaty armpits. "You know it's just about over Mr. Author Sir, over for me in this state you got me in, Ha, ha, ha! And soon it will begin for you in this same state. I, I, ha, ha, ha, I hope you're wearin' black socks for me as well...HARRRRRRRR!"

I arched my legs as far as they would go and I could feel the goop oozing from my slit even more as my armpits were meanly tickle tortured...

At exactly two minutes to the last hour Christopher stopped tickling my armpits and climbed off me. He stood at the side of the bed as I caught my breath, laying there bathed in sweat and bondage and black socks.

"You may as well start untying me now bud," I chuckled meanly. "For once I have won one of your predicament games and..."

"Like I said earlier, it's not over till its over," Christopher said, cutting me off in mid sentence.

Then, I watched as he picked up the electronic control for the danged butt plug that was still wedged and stretched in my shit chute.

"HAR, har for you buddy of mine, if you recall correctly that thing didn't work before," I laughed.

"Maybe it will now," Christopher said and I watched in horror as he slid a hand in his pants pocket and brought out a double AA battery.

"What in the fucks?" I whispered.

Smiling evilly Christopher inserted the missing battery in the electronic control device...

"Oh my word, oh my fucking fucks, you tricked me man," I whimpered, looking up at the clock...and saw that I had only a minute and a half to go. "Christopher you wouldn't..."

Without a word Christopher pressed a button on the electronic control and the buzzing that I had anticipated earlier started now in my danged shit chute...

"OOOOOOOOOOOOOOOO..." I groaned as it did indeed feel as if a swarm of bees was buzzing around in my hole.

My mid section lifted itself involuntarily off the bed. Oh was I sexy at that moment, all naked but for black OTC socks and muscular, bound tight in a spread eagle with my erection of steel pointing at my stomach area, oh my word! I sweated like crazy, I reeked like a guy in a locker room after a hard workout, and boy howdy had I been worked out buds. I clenched my bound hands into tight fists and curled my toes back under my black socks... My eyes opened wide as oodles of pre-seed emanated from my piss slit now...

"OOOOOOOOOO Christopher..." I moaned and I could feel my load of pent-up spunk churning and building in my balls. "NO, NO...I want to win man...I want to win..."

In response my tickle buddy pressed another button on the electronic control device. The buzzing intensified... My entire asshole was vibrating let me tell you... The walls of my chute seemed to clench tighter around the inflatable butt-plug that Christopher had wedged and stretched up inside me.

"One minute to go Timmy, sixty tiny seconds..." Christopher whispered.

"OOOOOOHHHHHHH, t-turn it off man, please..." I whimpered and looking down at my piss slit as it looked up at me I saw the beginnings of my gusher starting. "OH NO, no, good as that feels, no... no...nooooooo..."

And then it happened; my cock spewed forth a load the likes of which I had never known before. I came, shooting my load like a madman, writhing on that bed, straining and flexing my biceps and triceps in the tight bondage...and it happened within the last minute of what was to have been my hundred days of abstinence.

"AAAAAAWWWWWWWW!" was the sound I made as I arched my head back, clenched my fists, curled my toes in my socks and spewed and spewed my mess, without my cock even having been touched.

It seemed that having my asshole stimulated and being tied and tickled had done me in. My hot load of creamy soup splattered and landed all over my stomach region, my chest, my nipples, my pecs, I kept cumming, I kept shooting, it seemed like it would never end...

The sounds of a man in passion and pain at the same time filled the room...

Christopher watched me in awe, wonderment and total adoration...

"Oh yes, cum my laddy, cum...cum Timmy..." Christopher whispered as my globs of semen coated my upper body.

"AAAWWWWWWWW!" I cawed again, louder this time as my cock spit forth a few more torrents of my thick sexy jazz. "OH MY WORD...never have I cum with such force!"

"That's what one hundred days of not shooting your load will do to you my laddy," Christopher said softly, still watching as the last remnants of my mess erupted from me.

"AWWWWWWWW..." I wailed a bit softer now, as my erection started to go soft.

A few drizzles of cum seeped out of me and then the buzzing in my hole started to subside. I looked up and saw that Christopher was pressing a button on the electronic control. Then, the buzzing stopped altogether and the butt-plug deflated. I lay there heaving, gasping, and catching my breath as the thing slid slowly from my shit chute.

"Well buddy, I'm sure that felt beyond awesome, but as you can see you came before your hundred days of abstinence was up," Christopher chided me, hunkering down next to the bed at my upper torso.

"So I did, so I did," I said in a mixture of ecstasy and disappointment.

"And you know what that means," the author said and I gasped as he started trailing his tongue around in my mess of goop that was all over me.

I wriggled and wiggled on the bed, still tied tight as the sounds of slurping now filled the area as Christopher ate my mess of jazz off me. Watching him scoff down my juices seemed to spur me on and my cock started to stiffen yet again.

"Oh yes, I know what that means buddy," I reeled as Christopher's tongue was like a cow's tongue as it moved over me, him paying special attention to sucking my cum off my tits. "OHHHHHHHHHH... another hundred days of not shooting my danged load..."

Christopher chuckled and said, "I was thinking more along the lines of one hundred and fifty days this time my laddy..."

"WHAT?" I blubbered and then as he ate my mess off my torso Christopher grabbed a handful of my hardening manhood and began stroking. "OH MY WORD..."

CHUCK'S TICKLISH PLIGHT

Dedicated to: Wayne C. (for extra "Ticklish" pointers...)
Authors: Christopher Trevor, Wayne Colburn and Adam H.

Author's Note: Before I begin relating "Chuck's Ticklish Plight" I want to first thank my internet buddy "Adam H" for his support, ticklish imagination and inspiration over the time of our friendship. When he had sent me some "joke" pictures and I saw one of them in particular I somehow envisioned the guy depicted as being a tickle victim...

The way he is depicted, looking real gullible I think is part of what set my ticklish and evil imagination soaring. Now granted in the picture he was wearing a wedding band but for the purposes of this story he is not yet married to the young lady beside him, her name being Daisy for the purposes of the forthcoming tale. The setting where the picture was taken is also superb for a playful tickle abduction. It looks like a nice quiet area in the woods by a lake with some mountains in the background. It's the sort of place, very remote and out of the way where young lovers would think that no one would find them...how wrong Chuck is. So, with all these elements pulled together I, Christopher Trevor, (Author), Adam H. (Poet and writing consultant) and Wayne C. (for input and "Ticklish" pointers) give you our first writing collaboration entitled, "Chuck's Ticklish Plight."

The Story

It was a warm and sultry afternoon when Chuck, groom to be, found himself in the very oddest of situations. The sun was beating down warmly and almost affectionately it would have seemed on the somewhat handsome but definitely rugged and muscular bearded Southern guy and his fiancé Daisy. The young couple was lying side by side on a large sheet set up on the grass by the tip of the lake where they'd just shared an afternoon together having a romantic lunch.

"Oh Daisy, I just cain't believe that in less n' a week now you and me is gonna be man and wife baby," Chuck drawled passionately as he rolled over and wearing just a pair of black tight fitting spandex boxer shorts now lay atop his bride to be, his sexy spandex clad ass pointing up at the heavens as he squirmed sexily and boned up against

Daisy. "Like they used to say back in them olden golden days, we is gonna be hitched baby! Yee Haw!"

Underneath him and with her scrawny arms around his bull-sized neck Daisy looked adoringly upwards at her groom to be. She felt his hardness against her bikini (which for the record was about two sizes small for her) clad crotch and his manliness made her swoon.

"I know Chuck; it seems like only yesterday that you and me started a datin'" Daisy said breathlessly and kissed Chuck on his bearded chin. "Married, we're a gonna be *married* Chuck. Why...the word itself just gives me the willies and the a chillys when I says it..."

Daisy smiled a smile so wide and passionate that it stretched from ear to ear. She kissed Chuck again on his bearded chin and he saw tears of joy in her eyes. He considered himself beyond lucky to have met such a young lady who loved him the way she did. He only wished that she would let go of the "I want to wait for our wedding night" hogwash to get down and do the dirty nasty deed, as the Southern redneck guy referred to it.

"Yeah, I know what you mean Daisy girl; the time since we got engaged just seems to have flown by like an eagle..." Chuck drawled in a man's passion, the look of a wild animal in his eyes.

"We's gonna have a lovely life together Chuck," Daisy whispered.

Smiling with that same man's passion in his chestnut shaped dark eyes Chuck hefted himself upwards a bit to relieve the pressure on his stalked up erection in his spandex shorts. He had agreed; he had given Daisy his word that they would wait until their wedding night to do the deed. And seeing as the wedding date was now just days away he had purposely started saving himself up. He had not shot a load in nearly four to five whole days. By the time their wedding night rolled around Chuck figured he would be filling his bride with his good stuff all the live long night...as he so comically stated it. Looking down at his fiancé, thinking days ahead to their wedding night Chuck grinded his naked toes into the soft earth as he lay back down atop the woman he loved. She again swooned at the feeling of his iron-like stem when she felt it pulsing against her crotch. She was so glad that Chuck had agreed to wait until their wedding night to make love to her. The way she figured it she would be riding his manhood all the live long night...as Chuck usually said it. She ran her fingers through his thick black hair and kissed him lovingly and passionately on the lips, kissed him on his eyes and cheeks and then his lips again. Chuck held Daisy tight in his muscular arms and did his damned best to hold back the impending eruption. More than anything he didn't want to soil his spandex shorts with his man juices. The couple's picnic lunch basket finished over an hour ago or so lay beside them along with the small pile of Chuck's clothes. As they lay there hugging, snuggling and kissing each other neither of them heard the large van as it came to a halt down by the road.

As Chuck did his best to simply cuddle with Daisy his eyes rolled in his head and he jokingly howled like a werewolf. He was raised up on the palms of his huge hands, looking down at Daisy and then up at the sky as he howled again. Daisy giggled and marveled at the sight of the colossal muscles in his arms. His biceps were the size of bowling balls and she loved how they seemed to flex involuntarily. His huge chest, what she called his rock hard male cleavage stared down at her, his chest adorned with two of the fleshiest and meatiest man nipples she had ever seen. Daisy swooned and her head spun as Chuck again held her in those huge arms of his, feeling his steel-like manhood pressing against her crotch. It amazed Daisy how Chuck's cock was always erect. He didn't seem to ever be soft in the private's area. His jeans seemed to always be tented with his erection. Sometimes maybe he thought she didn't notice that, but she did, she sure as hell did. She figured she was marrying a twenty-four hour a day sex machine. She gasped for breath in his tight masculine embrace. Chuck leaned down further and kissed Daisy on one of her bikini covered erect nipples. She whispered his name breathlessly as he kissed and tongued her nipple through her bikini top. It was one of the small favors she had granted him. On their wedding night he swore that he would suck her tits right off her chest, that's how horned he would be... As Daisy moaned sweetly and as Chuck howled again like a werewolf neither of them heard the sounds of the doors of the van opening and then closing. The driver stepped stealthily from his seat and his buddy, a guy named Sam stepped down from the passenger seat. The driver's other buddies, Jack and Victor stepped out from the back seat. The four burly men stretched their legs and looked upwards at the area where Chuck and Daisy were having their afternoon romantic lunch. The four men smiled fiendishly, donned ski masks and started making their way toward their prey...

After Chuck and Daisy finally let go of each other they sat up. Sitting there in her two sizes small for her bikini Daisy watched as Chuck dressed, pulling on his black tee shirt and then his black gym shorts over his tight spandex ones.

"I suppose we best be headin' on a home at this point Daisy," Chuck said as he sat getting his socks on.

"Yeah, I suppose we should at that," Daisy replied, adjusting her bikini top as she spoke. "I'm a glad I came here a wearin' this here bikini. I enjoyed the swim earlier... Watching you swim all sexy like in them there spandex shorts of yours really set my heart a racing."

"Glad you appreciated the show baby, you all didn't look all that bad in that there sexy bikini you're a wearin'" Chuck drawled, the look of a man stupefied by love etched on his face as he pulled his first sock on. "Good thing that these sexy spandexes of mine dried up though Daisy...wouldn't want to show up at home with wet lookin' unnerwears on now..."

While Chuck was sitting, looking lovingly at his fiancé with one sock on and the other held in hand ready to be put on his other foot the driver of the van, Sam, Jack and Victor had made their way silently and slowly to the picnic area. Neither Chuck nor Daisy were the wiser for what was about to happen. The four men quickly huddled behind a large bush. The driver whispered instructions to his three buddies and then they were off and running at top speed toward Chuck and Daisy, just as Chuck was pulling his other gray ribbed sweat sock on.

"Well, I guess we best start a headin' on back then eh Daisy baby?" Chuck asked again and as he pulled his sock up, his back turned to the four approaching men, looked into his fiancé's adoring eyes. He saw her look of adoration suddenly turn to a look of terror.

"Hey, whassamatter baby?" Chuck asked.

"OH MY GOD, Chuck!" Daisy screamed loudly as Chuck was reaching for his sneakers and she involuntarily gripped the back of his huge neck with one hand.

Suddenly, as he sat there on the grass, from behind him Chuck felt his socked ankles grabbed and he was being pulled roughly and meanly from his fiancé's grip, him sliding on his stomach on the grass.

"H-HEY! HEY! WHAT THE FUCKING FUCK?" Chuck snarled as his feet were then hoisted a few inches off the ground and he was dragged further away from Daisy, yet she held tight to his strong neck.

"CHUCK, what's a goin' on?" Daisy screamed.

She held to Chuck's big neck for as long as possible but then, as the van driver and Sam dragged him off her by his socked ankles her hold was snagged off. Chuck then held to Daisy's legs, his body squirming as he was dragged roughly further in the grass by his ankles. When he was unable to hold onto her any longer he was pulled away from his loving fiancé.

"HEY you fucking assholes, leggo of my danged feet!" Chuck snarled like a trapped bear as he managed to turn his head to see the ski masked men as they dragged him along on the grass. "FUCKING fucks, who the hell are you jokers and what is this shit?"

"OH MY GOD, Chuck, what do they want? What do they want baby? Who are they?" Daisy screamed as when she tried to get to her feet she was dutifully grabbed by the arms by Jack and Victor.

They pulled her upwards till she was standing between the two men. They held her firmly by her scrawny arms and she watched helplessly and with her heart rending as her fiancé pounded his huge fists against the grass as he was dragged further away.

"Let's go honey," Jack said to Daisy, disguising his voice, as he and Victor began moving her along. "You and your brawny fiancé there onna the ground are about to receive your first weddin' present, yuk, yuk, yuk and yum!"

"You let go of me, and you two unhand Chuck!" Daisy screamed.

The driver of the van and Sam, each holding Chuck by one of his socked ankles walked along the grass back toward their van, Chuck's legs raised high as he was dragged along helplessly, not in any position whatsoever to be of any use to himself or his terrified fiancé.

"How, how do you know we's getting married?" Daisy fumed as she kicked her legs forward as the two men half carried and half dragged her along.

Looking down she watched miserably as Chuck tried to pull himself free of the driver's and Sam's awful tight grips on his ankles. Chuck dug his long fingers into the dirt and tried to get a grip, hoping it would cause the two men to lose their hold on him, sadly it was for naught.

"Let's just say we know of your impending nuptials and leave it at that eh honey, honey?" Jack replied. "Yuk, yuk, yuk and yum!"

"You bastards, you fucking shit heads!" Chuck snarled from the ground as the driver of the van and Sam now faced forward as they walked along, Chuck's ankles raised high off the ground and under their strong arms. "You guys leggo of Daisy! I swear by all that's holy and all that's not if you as much as lay a finger on her I'll kill ya! I'll kill ya to death that's what I'll do, I swear that I will!"

By now Chuck was moving along on the palms of his huge hands, practically being carried along by the driver and Sam.

"What in the fucking fucks is this all about?" Chuck garbled. "What the hell kinda weddin' present could four lowlife kidnappers have for us?"

"Chuck, please...do somethin' please..." Daisy pleaded as Jack held her arm tight with one hand and grabbed a handful of her chunky ass with the other.

"PERVERT! Get your filthy paws offen my fiancé!" Chuck ranted miserably, pounding the grass with his fists, his macho pride feeling horribly deflated at not being able to help Daisy.

When Daisy saw the parked van she let out a blood curdling scream. The horrid realization that she and her fiancé *were* about to be kidnapped hit her hard, consumed her almost.

"OH GOD, what do you rascals want from us?" Daisy shrieked as they were herded toward the opened back doors of the large van.

"It ain't much we want from you lady, lady," Victor giggled, he also disguising his voice when he spoke, sounding like a sadistic school boy as he forced Daisy along. "But your fiancé there on the ground is soon gonna learn the first tribulations o' bein' a hubby..."

From the other side of her as he dragged her along Jack said,

"Yuk, yuk, yuk, and yum…"

"WH-what do you mean? What tribulations? Chuck, what do they want from you baby?" Daisy squealed.

When they reached the back of the van Daisy was the first to see the huge thick net dangling from the ceiling of the inside of it. It looked like it was supported by two strong nail-bolts of some kind. The driver of the van and Sam grabbed Chuck's socked ankles tighter and literally hoisted him up off the ground in an upside down position. Chuck's arms flailed out uselessly.

"OHHHHHRRRR FUCKING fuckers put me down you guys!" Chuck roared as he waved his arms helplessly.

Daisy screamed again as she watched her fiancé as he was hoisted into the van and then deposited bodily into the giant net, as if he were a large caught fish. Chuck let out a loud huffing sound and a smelly fart as he became tangled up in the dangling net. His muscled weight caused the net to hang down a bit and then he was hanging in it in the back of the van. The men all laughed at the sound and scent of Chuck's fart.

"OH FUCKING fucks, I'm all a trapped and tied up in this danged net Daisy!" Chuck grumbled as he struggled to no avail.

"I'll tell ya buddy boy, you struggle, you struggle real good up there ya hear?" the driver laughed, disguising his voice as his buddies had done already. "Because I'll tell ya Chucky ol' Chuckles, the more you struggle the more tangled up in that net you'll be…"

"WHO the fuck are you guys?" Chuck screamed from within his netted prison.

It was when Daisy screamed the words, "NO, NO, don't do that!" that Chuck's attention was suddenly riveted to his fiancé. Looking down from where he was trapped and dangling he saw that the two men who had her in their grip were now busy tying her up.

"HEY, leave her alone you bastards!" Chuck pleaded as he watched them tie Daisy's hands behind her and her naked feet together at the ankles. "Don't be tyin' her up you bastards! OH GOD, DAISY! Daisy!"

"Chuck, make 'em stop, oh no, they's a tyin me up Chuck,' Daisy screamed frantically.

When they were done tying her Jack meanly slid two fingers down the front of Daisy's bikini bottom and gave her pussy a quick flick.

"OHHHHHHHH!" Daisy panted and then she was hoisted up into the back of the van along with her poor trapped fiancé.

"You bastard, I'll getcha for that..." Chuck threatened as he watched the men sit Daisy on the floor of the van, a few feet from where he was trapped and hanging in the net.

"Now you two behave yourselves back here for the duration of the ride ya hear?" Victor laughed.

"Where you takin' us?" Chuck asked angrily as he struggled in the net, the confines of it snaring him tighter and tighter in its mesh.

"You'll see soons enough," the driver said and grinned in his ski mask.

The grin looked somehow familiar to Chuck but with the state that his mind was in he could not put his finger on why. The back doors of the van were slammed shut and only the light from the sultry afternoon through the two small windows on the doors lighted the interior now.

"OH GOD, oh Chuck, we, we been kidnapped..." Daisy said,

crying now, terrified. "What do they want from us Chuck? It cain't be ransom they a want... We's ain't rich, we's ain't rich by a short long shot..."

"Now you hush Daisy, we's got to figure some way outen this mess," Chuck rasped. "FUCKING fucks, lookit how they got me all netted and packaged up here, fucking totally fucks..."

They heard the sounds of the four men climbing into the front section of the van and then the van started moving along the road. Daisy cried harder... The only evidence that Chuck and Daisy had been at the lip of the lake were their lunch basket, the sheet they had been lying on and Chuck's sneakers, which he had not gotten onto his feet before his abduction... "I'm a scared Chuck," Daisy whimpered.

"Daisy, Daisy, listen to me baby..." Chuck panted, his fingers gripping the tiny holes of the net he dangled in. "You're in a better position than me to get free, ya hear?"

"WH-what?" Daisy asked, sniveling.

"Somehow baby, somehow, you gots to get untied Daisy," Chuck panted. "You gots to get untied and then get me outen this here net they lifted me into...I cain't do jack shit in the position they got me in up heres! Double damn man! And remember what that joker said, iffen I struggle in this danged net the more tangled up I'll get! You got more leverage freedom down there than I do up here..."

"H-how am I supposed to get free?" Daisy asked miserably. "The way they gotten me all tied tight like I cain't move..."

Chuck mulled on it for a moment and then his eyes lit up, the way Daisy loved it, his eyes lit up. Looking up at her trapped fiancé Daisy suddenly felt a tingling and a slight wetness at her crotch.

"Daisy, the floor of the van is metal right?" Chuck asked, sounding desperate.

"I-I suppose so it is, why?" Daisy asked.

"Lie down on your back and feel around for a sharp edge," Chuck said instructionally. "When you find a sharp edge start a rubbing the ropes around your wrists against it."

"Oh, oh yes, good idea Chuck," Daisy said happily and did as her fiancé said.

Watching her squirm on the floor of the van Chuck then felt a tingling at his crotch too... He could not seem to take his eyes off watching how her tits jiggled in her bikini top and her crotch squiggled around as she squirmed on the floor of the van.

That's a it Daisy, that's it baby, we's gonna be okay, we's gonna get outen this, you mark my words baby..." Chuck drawled happily as his erection pounded in his shorts.

After a while Daisy was half standing as she leaned against one of the side walls of the van, rubbing her wrists there, trying now to find a sharp edge along the wall. As the van plowed on she was jostled and nearly lost her balance. She stumbled and her face landed against the side of Chuck's crotch in his netted prison. She involuntarily took a deep breath and the scent of musty sweat emanating from her fiancé's most private area filled her nostrils. She shuddered in ecstasy and returned to the task at hand of trying to find a sharp edge to break her bonds with. She leaned back against the other side wall of the van. After a long while Daisy found a sharp edge and began sliding the rope tied around her wrists against it. It was slow and tedious work. As she tried her best to get untied Daisy was again knocked against her dangling fiancé. This time her nose collided with one of his ass cheeks...

The van came to a halt about a half hour later in front of a large cabin set by itself in an isolated area of the wooded road. Two more men, Chris and Adam looked out the window of the cabin.

"They're here, *fuck*, I can't believe it, they really did it, it looks like," Chris said to Adam and the two men looked at the large oak table dominating the center of the cabin and all the rope piled up next to that table.

"They have to have done it," Adam added. "If they didn't they wouldn't be back here..."

Outside the cabin the driver of the van and his three cohorts disembarked from the vehicle and headed towards the back of it.

"I want him blindfolded from here on out," the driver said sternly. "It's too damned hot to keep these ski masks on while we work ol' Chuckle Chuck over."

"But then Daisy will see who we are man..." Jack said. "And you said that half the fun of this was them not knowing who it was that nabbed them...Maybe we should blindfold her too."

"I don't give a rat's ass if Daisy knows who we are..." the driver said as they sidled up to the back doors of the van. "She cain't be blindfolded, seeing as we *want* her to watch while her fiancé gets his before the wedding present. If she decides to give us away to her soon to be blindfolded beau then "he" suffers more...it's that simple...the choice is hers really..."

"Yuk, yuk, yuk and yum, you think of everything man..." Jack snickered as the driver opened the van doors. "HOLY SHIT!"

"OH NO!" Daisy screamed as she was still working at trying to get Chuck freed from the net after having taken an inordinate amount of time to get herself freed first.

"She's loose, she's fucking loose!" the driver barked angrily. "Grab her before she frees..."

But, as the driver was about to end his sentence Daisy managed to get the ends of the net untied and Chuck rolled free of the binding mesh.

"FUCK!" the driver yelled. "Get them!"

"CHUCK!" Daisy screamed as her fiancé was getting himself to his socked feet and she was dutifully grabbed by Jack and Victor and hustled roughly out of the van, her breasts almost falling free of her bikini. "CHUCK!"

"Come on Daisy baby, yuk, yuk, yuk and yum," Jack trilled meanly.

"LEGGO of my fiancé you perverts!" Chuck reeled and came plowing out of the van like a madman.

With his enormously muscular arms outstretched he reached for the driver's neck, only to be ambushed from behind by Sam. Sam meanly kicked Chuck's legs out from under him, sending the groom sprawling.

"AAARRRRHHH no man..." Chuck garbled as the driver then reached down to grab his wrists.

He hauled poor Chuck upwards to his socked feet, dancing him around stupidly in the grass.

"You ain't getting outa this all that easily buddy boy..." the driver said and as Chuck struggled in his grasp the driver pulled Chuck close to him and pecked the groom to be on the cheek.

"SLOB!" Chuck spat in the guy's ski masked face and as his fiancé watched helplessly the driver lifted Chuck over his shoulders in a fireman's carry so that his arms and legs were pinned as he was then lugged toward the cabin.

Perched up there on the huge man's shoulders Chuck looked

down at his fiancé as the other two men moved her along toward the cabin as well. Chuck's cock was (fear) hard in his shorts.

"Daisy, Daisy, *I swear*, I have no idea what the fucking fucks they want baby..." Chuck called out helplessly. "I have no clue what this is all about Daisy!"

As they walked into the cabin Chris and Adam quickly donned their ski masks and then turned to the other four men and their captives.

"Shit, shit, thanks so much for the help out there you two!" the driver grumbled at Chris and Adam. "It would have been real fun chasing these two through the woods had they gotten away huh? You saw us struggling with them! The bitch somehow got untied in the van and nearly caused us to lose the groom! Why didn't you two come out and help us round them back up again?"

"You seemed to be doin' okay out there," Adam said with a fiendish looking grin on his ski masked face as he approached the driver, taking in the sight of Chuck draped and pinned over his shoulders.

"Man, you really did manage to snag him," Adam said, grinned over at his buddy Chris and snapped the elastic in one of Chuck's socks as he lay across the muscleman driver's shoulders.

"Let me down you bastard!" Chuck ranted and realized how the men's conversations all pointed to the fact that they had wanted *him* especially in their clutches and not really Daisy. "And tell that guy to leave my danged socks alone huh?"

"Get his pesky fiancé tied to a chair and lets get this side of beef prepared for his wedding present..." the driver said and slammed Chuck down on the huge oak table on his back.

"UHHHHHHH!" Chuck grunted as his back hit the table.

He tried to quickly get up off the table but his arms and ankles were grabbed by Chris, Adam, the driver and Sam. Chuck was held tight and fast in a spread eagle sort of position as he watched helplessly while Jack and Victor lashed his bikinied girlfriend to a straight back chair.

"What in Sam hell do you bastards want? Talk to me here!" Chuck grumbled as he squirmed in the four men's grasps.

"Okay, she's goin' nowhere soon, lets get started on our groom over there, yuk, yuk, yuk and yum," Jack joked when he and Victor were done tying Daisy to the chair.

While the driver, Sam, Chris and Adam held Chuck tight Jack and Victor began stripping their victim.

"H-hey, HEY! What are you perverts up to here?" Chuck crowed loudly as his shirt was pushed up and over his arms, baring his huge hairy muscular chest and two of the fattest and plumpest nipples any of the guys had ever seen.

"Damn, double damn, he's got better fucking tits than some women I've dated..." Chris stated and gave one of Chuck's jutted up nipples a squeeze and twist.

"HEY, what are you guys faggots?" Chuck spat up at Chris as his spandex shorts and the ones over them were being pulled down his legs toward his socked feet. "Keep your hands off my danged tits buddy boy!"

The men all snickered gleefully as Chuck's shorts and spandex were taken off him...

"DAMN, he's stalked up to full mast," Jack said, reaching over and grabbing a handful of Chuck's manhood, twirling the monster-sized cock in his fist.

"FUCKER, DANGED SICKO! Leggo my cock man!" Chuck panted as Adam did the honors of peeling the angry groom's socks off his feet. "Fucking guys are a handlin' me like I was some Saturday night proteetute or something there abouts..."

"Looks to me likes he's really enjoyin' all this huh guys?" Jack asked as he whirled Chuck's hard crust some more. "Yuk, yuk, yuk, and yum..."

Chuck's eyes rolled in his head as he felt the crown of his cock tingle and his stored up man juices cooked hotly in his kiwi-sized balls... He knew that just a tad more and whoever the fuck this guy was that had his erection in hand would have him spewing what could very well be the first of many hefty loads.

A short while later Chuck was tied to the table on his back, his muscular arms pulled up and over his head, his hands joined at the wrists, tied tightly together and the short slack of the rope extended over and tied off to one of the table legs. His legs were spread wide across the table and his ankles were each tied off to one of the table legs at the other side.

"Damn it all Daisy, lookits the way they got me all trussed up here like some Thanksgivin' turkey and whatnot!" Chuck groaned and squirmed miserably, his cock embarrassingly erect, his head turned and looking at Daisy as she struggled tied to the chair.

Then, a black cloth was placed over Chuck's eyes, effectively blindfolding him...

"HEY, oh no, no, why this too?" Chuck drawled, sounding panicky. "Coverin' up my danged eyes..."

"Welcome to your first of what I'm sure will be many wedding presents Chuck ol' boy," the van driver said as he and the other five of the groom's captors began pulling off their ski masks.

"OH MY LORD!" Daisy cried out when she saw the van driver's face, along with the other men's faces as well. "Y-YOU! Oh my God, all of you!"

"Now Daisy, you keep that trap of yours shut," the driver said, holding up a finger and pointing at the helpless bride to be. "You say a word and your handsome fiancé here suffers even more of what we plan on skirtin' him through..."

"And just what the fucking fucks are you all plannin' on skirtin' me through pray tell?" Chuck said loudly, looking around in blindfolded darkness. "I suppose that kidnappin' me and Daisy wasn't enough for you mugs eh?"

Suddenly, the cabin was filled with the sound of loud and raucous laughter as the six men tickle tortured the tied down groom. The driver of the van and Sam had taken up position at Chuck's armpits and were digging their fingers in deep, twirling them in his cavernous pits. They were even strumming their fingertips up and down and up and down some more in the groom's moist and sweaty armpits...

To be sure, Chuck was astounded at this atypical and most unusual turn of events... He could not believe, that of all things, they were tickle torturing him...

Jack and Victor stood on either side of the table tickling Chuck's ribs and sides, making him squirm in his bondage like a fish out of water atop the table he lay on... Jack had added a torturous feather to the mix, tickling the tip of Chuck's cock head with it as he tickled his ribs and sides with his other hand... Adam and Chris were each squatting at one of Chuck's tied up bare feet. They were each lick tickling the bottom of one of the groom to be's meaty big feet, sliding and slathering their tongues up and down and up and down in a gliding and very ticklish manner...

"OHHHHHHHHHHH HOO, HOO, HOO, HOO, HOO, HOO, oh my Gawd Daisy, I'm, I'm a bein' a tickle tortured here...of all things honey,

honey..." Chuck hyena laughed behind his blindfold. "HAR, HAR, HAR, untie me you bastards, I-let me fucking loose! HO, HO, HO, g-got me imitatin' Santa Claus here, HO, HO, HO!"

"Yeah, it sure does a sound like Santa Claus is comin' to town, yuk, yuk, yuk and yum," Jack laughed as he feathered the tip of Chuck's erection and finger tickled his ribs and side.

"HAR, HAR, HAR," Chuck cackled. "You mugs'll pay for this shit!"

"Pay for it?" the van driver asked and dug his fingers deeper into the trapped groom's armpit that he was tickle torturing. "Chuckles ol' boy my groom to be, we're not payin' for shit here! We're getting it all for free!"

"HAHAHA!" Chuck screamed his laughter. "S-STOP ticklin' me you all shit heads! Oh my Gods please stop..."

"Stop it, stop it," Daisy panted from where she sat tied up. "He's very tickle sensitive! He can't take that!"

"Oh he'll take it Daisy, he'll take it for sure," the van driver laughed sadistically. "Call this his initiation to being a married man. "And thank you Daisy dear for bringing it to our evil attention that your fiancé here is so danged tickle sensitive."

"Yuk, yuk, yuk and yum, but that just makes me want to tickle the life out of him even more..." Jack piped up.

As Chuck laughed and squirmed atop the table his cock bobbed and twitched back and forth, swaying in the wind like a flag on a pole it would have seemed.

"HAH, HAH, HAH," Chuck ranted in laughter. "D-Daisy, I can feel two of 'em thar perverts lickin' and ticklin' my danged stanky feet, talk about slobs! Ha, ha, ha, ha!"

"And just for the records Chuckles ol' Chuck," the van driver said, leaning down and speaking directly into the captive's ear. "What we're doing to you here is only the beginning. We have a slew, *a fucking slew* of devices that we plan to use on you to tickle the livin' daylights out of you..."

"HAHAHA!" WH-why in Sam hell are you all a doin' this to me?" Chuck panted.

What he really wanted to ask was why they were doing it to him and not to Daisy. Of course the muscular groom would never want to see his fiancé harmed in any way...or tickle tortured for that matter. But wouldn't most men who'd gotten the drop on a couple want to torment the female half of that couple? *Wouldn't they?* Chuck wondered as he laughed and laughed. But in this case the joke was apparently on him but he just didn't get the joke. But for a guy who didn't get the joke he sure as all hell was laughing at the unknown punch line.

"You'll find out soon enough Chuckles," the van driver laughed and twirled his fingers in Chucks' now very sweaty armpit while Sam did the same with the other one.

"When, when you boys, ha, ha, ha, ha, when you boys kidnapped me and a Daisy we thought we was bein' nabbed for, HAW, HAW, HAW, nabbed for ransom!" Chuck managed to drawl.

"Not as simple as that my groom to be," the van driver said into the captive's ear.

All Chuck could do was laugh and laugh and laugh and sweat bullets atop the table...

His cock throbbed huge and beefy between his legs as Jack went on and on feathering the tip of it...

The feelings emanating from his feet as Chris and Adam lick

tickled them sent chills up his tree trunks like legs and through his very being… His cock tingled some more as the two guys really licked, licked, and licked his bare feet.

"What a weddin' present you six are a givin' us," Daisy prattled angrily, looking especially over at the van driver. "Wait'll poor Chuck is untied. He'll make short work of all of you…"

"I seriously doubt that Daisy darlin'" the van driver laughed and then leaned down and started tonguing the fuck out of Chuck's smelly and rancid armpit.

"YAHHHHHHHHHH!" Chuck screamed anew.

"Oh poor Chuck…" Daisy cried pitifully.

A short while later all six men switched spots when it came to tickling their captured groom to be…

The van driver and Sam were now at Chuck's bare feet. Sam was busily sucking one of Chuck's big toes as he finger tickled the bottom of his foot while the van driver tickled the bottom and arch of Chuck's other foot. It seemed that the tickling of Chuck's arch was sending the groom to be over the edge as his laughter grew louder and more pronounced each time said arch was tickled.

Jack and Victor were tickling Chuck's armpits, Jack alternating using his fingers and the feather that he had used on Chuck's huge and pulsing erection. Victor was digging into Daisy's fiancé's armpit like he was digging for gold, sending searing ticklish sensations through the guy, making him HEE HAW his laughter crazily…

Chris and Adam took up position at Chuck's sides and tickle tortured his sides and ribs…

"Man, tickling a guy is great huh?" Chris asked his new buddy.

"Yeah, and we haven't even gotten to the devices yet..." Adam replied, glancing over at the video camera that he had set up on a tripod. "Or the jar..."

Adam fiendishly thought how the video of Chuck's tickle torments would be a superb birthday gift for him. Of course Adam would always keep a copy of it where Chuck could never get it, just for insurance purposes of course...

"HAR, HAR, HAR! Sons of bitches, monsters!" Chuck laughed loudly. "Daisy, one of 'em is suckin' and a sucklin' my danged big toe! "HAHAHA!"

"I knows it Chuck; I ain't blindfolded like you are..." Daisy said and all the men, at her comment, joined in Chuck's laughter then.

As Chuck laughed and laughed and sweated like mad his cock was throbbing and stalked up between his spread legs. Pre cum and beads of piss emanated from his wide sexy slit.

Looking at her tied down laughing fiancé Daisy suddenly felt her own juices flowing against her bikini bottom. She wondered miserably how the van driver could so such a thing to poor Chuck... At that thought her juices flowed more liberally...

As Chuck's rock hardness pointed straight up at heaven (or the ceiling of the cabin, which ever you prefer) Jack took that opportunity to tease and tickle the groom's cock slit. He wedged the tip of the feather into Chuck's gaping piss hole and twirled the device meanly round and round.

"YAHHHHHHHHH!" Chuck screamed, even though the rest of the assembled guys had stopped tickling their captured prey at that point.

"Oh you pervert whoever you are, DOUBLE DRAT and all a that!" Chuck railed. "HAW, HAW, HAW! I-I'm a so horned up like nobody's danged business! HAHAHA! I been a savin' myself just for Daisy for when we gets married in a few more days! Ha, ha, ha, ha, FUCKING FUCKS ME, but I'm hornier than a cat in heat on a hot summer night! HAHAHA!"

"Then it sure as all hell is a good thing I brought this jar with me when I decided to join in on this ticklish venture..." Adam said and Jack stopped tickling Chuck's piss hole.

"WH-what jar? What is Sam hell do you mean fucker?" Chuck garbled, grimacing behind his blindfold as Adam took his cock in hand. "AW GEEZ, Daisy darlin', one of 'em perverts has got me by the cock now baby!"

Daisy inwardly seethed as she watched Adam handling her fiancé's most private body part. Chuck pursed his lips tightly together and tried in vain to fend off the feelings that were boiling inside him, and boiling in his balls as well as Adam began a slow rhythmic stroking on his skin flute. All at once Chuck didn't need an explanation for the "jar" that Adam had just mentioned, but he listened anyway as Adam explained.

"I got here an empty eight ounce jelly jar Chuck ol' boy," Adam laughed, holding Chuck's pulsing manhood straight out and aimed at the mouth of the jar. "Every time we tickle you to a state of oblivion we're gonna milk this udder of yours. Lets see how full you can get this jar, hardy, har, har buddy..."

"And yuk, yuk, yuk and yum..." Jack chuckled.

"NO, NO, stop that now!" Chuck ranted. "Ticklin' the livin' day and night lights outten me is one thing, but milkin' my danged muscle pipe is a horse of a totally 'nother color you bastard, whoever the fucks you are! OHHHRRRRRRRR, fucking fucks fucker, leggo my manhood! I been storin' up my sticky stuff just for Daisy..."

"Horse of another color is right, seeing as your cock is horse sized," Adam chuckled as he stroked Chuck's mammoth sized penis.

"Aw c'mon man, don't be milkin' me here like some farm cow..." Chuck gasped, his head raised up off the table momentarily as he panted breathlessly.

But as he prattled on and on there was no denying that the groom to be was about to shoot a load the likes of which he'd never had before...

"And did you know, that most guys, after they cum are even more tickle sensitive somehow?" Jack asked Chuck and squeezed one of his nipples as Victor squeezed the guy's other nipple, sending chills and thrills through the groom to be. "Yuk, yuk, yuk and yum..."

Adam used Chucks' slithering pre cum as a lubricant as it oozed from his wide slit and snaked down the sides of his pulsing shaft. The sounds of squishing filled the cabin as Adam expertly stroked Chuck's cock. Under his blindfold Chuck's eyes rolled in his head.

"AWWWWWWW man, dang it all, I'm a close now you pervert," Chuck grunted and then a few seconds later the tied down muscle headed groom let fly with a potent geyser of sperm. "AAAAAAAAAHHHHHHHH! FUCKING fucks fucker! Got me creamin' my danged load here!"

The groom to be's cum splashed and jettisoned into the jar, making plopping sounds as it landed within.

"AAAAAAAAHHHHHHRRR SHIT, crappy thing to do to a groom in waitin' you asshole!" Chuck panted.

He shuddered in a state of ecstasy mixed with rage as he seemed to cum and cum.

"Damn, you really have been storin' it up buddy," Adam chuckled as he went on stroking and milking Chuck's cock, squeezing every possible drop of his mess out of him as the other guys whooped it up and cheered him on. "If this was a shootin' gallery you would have won first prize here buddy boy."

"Yuk, yuk, yuk and yum," Jack said. "I'll second that..."

"That was for Daisy on our weddin' night fool," Chuck drawled breathlessly then when he was done shooting his load.

"Oh I'm sure you'll be able to cook up more of your good stuff in those huge balls of yours come your wedding night old man," Adam chuckled meanly.

As Chuck's cock went semi flaccid and rested against his spent sweaty balls Daisy looked in envy at the jar that contained her fiancé's love juices, seething all the more. She thought how if she hadn't made Chuck wait for their wedding night that potent load of milk could have been hers...should have rightly been hers. Adam screwed the lid on the jar and placed it on a nearby shelf. The way Chuck's cum slimed down the sides of the jar somehow made Daisy's own juices slime in her bikini.

"Okay, now warm him up for the box", the van driver said with authority in his voice as he stepped over to Daisy.

The other five men resumed "tickle duty" on their captive and once more the cabin was filled with the sound of Chuck's helpless and raucous laughter. As the groom laughed the driver of the van hunkered down next to the tied up Daisy.

"You see that box under the table Daisy darlin'?" the driver asked her. "That mechanical gizmo is the first device up for grabs that we're a gonna use to tickle that hairy groom of yours all the more. "And I want you narrating for us when we start it on him...or on his big smelly feet I should say, just to be more pre-cise..."

Daisy looked at the van driver in disbelief and then back over at her being tickled, tied down and blindfolded fiancé.

"HAW, HAW, HAW," Chuck cackled loudly. "Oh Gawd Daisy, whoever that character is was right! After a poor sap of a guy shoots his load, HAHAHA, he, he's even more danged ticklish somehow!"

Daisy almost jumped from her seat when the van driver tweaked one of her nipples under her still slightly wet bikini top...

"D-Daisy, HAW, HAW, HAW, oh woe is me baby, but I'm really more danged ticklish now somehow..." Chuck panted as the guy's tickled his armpits, his sides and ribs, his stomach region and of course his bare feet and toes.

"This is a mean thing you guys are a doin' to poor Chuck," Daisy said to the van driver as he got to his feet.

"You mean a fun thing Daisy darlin'," the driver said and stepped back over to the table. "Okay you mugs, it's time for the "box."

"WH-WHAT box?" Chuck laughed. "WHAT FUCKING fucked up box?"

The Box

Chuck lay atop the table sweating and catching his breath as his six captors prepared for the next piece de résistance, namely the next session of tickle torture that the groom to be would endure. As he lay there still tied down tight Jack held the groom's blindfolded head up under one arm as he fed him a bottle of mineral water. Chuck sipped the cool water down gratefully, his Adam's apple bobbing sexily in his big neck, his cock almost up at full mast again between his muscular legs. What the groom to be did not know was that Jack had laced the mineral water with a chopped up hundred milligram Viagra pill.

"There ya go ya love sick fool," Jack said as he fed Chuck the water, glancing over at the tied up groom's fiancé. "Yuk, yuk, yuk and yum, cain't have you dehydrating on us now can we?"

"I'll reckon not," Chuck said in between sips of water.

Jack kissed Chuck on his cheek as Daisy watched her man being fed the water, her also unaware of the fact that the water contained an aphrodisiac. She felt her juices staining her bikini bottom as she watched Chuck's helplessness and his hardness twitching upwards. She had to wonder what it was about seeing her fiancé all tied up, blindfolded and being tickle tormented that seemed to be really getting her, her jollies that is...

"Okay boys, its time for the first item up for grabs," the van driver announced then, reached under Chuck's table and held up the medium sized wooden box that was under there.

Daisy took in the fact that there were two large round holes cut into one of the sides of the box, while at the other sides were numerous buttons and dials. Somehow she knew that she didn't need three guesses to know what the inside of the box contained. In blindfolded darkness Chuck heard the sound of a smaller table being sidled up at the foot of the one he was tied to. His cock throbbed and even though he had shot a load he felt even hornier than he'd had before he'd cum. He had to wonder at that. At the same time he felt his bare feet being untied and then his ankles grabbed and held tightly immobilized by Chris and Adam.

"D-Daisy, what are they doing pray tell?" Chuck garbled.

"Yes Daisy, why don't you tell your handsome beau here just what it is we're doing?" the van driver asked Daisy snidely, glancing sexily over at the recording video camera.

Daisy fumed as she looked at the van driver and the video camera as it recorded the incriminating evidence.

"They, they're a settin' up a small table at your feet Chuck," Daisy sniveled breathlessly, really looking at her fiancé's big bare feet for the first time it seemed, really drinking in the sight of them.

For the first time ever all Daisy wanted at that moment was to be all over Chuck's enormous feet, servicing them with every nuance of her being. She imagined licking the great meaty bottoms of them and she dribbled her juices in her bikini bottom. Her erect nipples pressed against her bikini top. She wondered why oh why she had made Chuck wait till they were getting married. She imagined flicking the tips of her erect nipples over Chuck's long toes and heat seemed to sluice through her fibers. She was so pumped with jealousy that one of the guys had sucked Chuck's big penis-like toe. Why was she thinking these things now, of all times, when she should have been thinking of a way to prevent what was about to happen to her poor groom she could not get her arms around.

"And uh, th-there's some sort of wooden box like device that they gots and they's a puttin' that box on the table at your feet," Daisy went on and felt her throat constrict as a large dollop of pre cum oozed from her fiancé's hard cock head and slithered down the shaft of it. "The box Chuck, it has two wide round holes in it...and..."

As Daisy spoke to her blindfolded beau Chris and Adam did the honors of sliding Chuck's big feet into the two holes in the box to just above his ankles. They slid covers around Chuck's feet and snapped them shut, thus preventing the studly guy from pulling his feet out.

"Oh Geez Daisy, I think they just a slided my big ol' feet into that box you're a describin' there to me baby," Chuck ranted miserably through clenched teeth. "And lo and fucking behold baby, this here gets worse on a count of I cain't yank my feet back out... What is this shit?"

"Well, there are uh, all sorts of dials and buttons on the sides of the box that your feet are in Chuck," Daisy said just as miserably, knowing all too well what was about to happen to her intended's feet in the box, knowing inwardly that the poor guy knew as well.

"Okay Chucky ol' Chuckles, it's your turn to recite a bit for us now," the van driver said and placed a finger against one of the buttons on the box. "Tell us, just so we know that we're all on the same page here...ha, just like those high classy New York executives say, just so we're all on the same page here...tell us what you feel at the bottoms of your big ol' bare feet in that box that you cain't rightly see..."

The man spoke sadistically yet comically...

"Oh geez man, this is a shitty way to treat a poor guy who's about to be takin' the marriage plunge," Chuck said sorrowfully as he felt his cock grabbed and twirled. "UHHHHHHHH...I-I think, I reckon, I feel the tops of brushes in that danged box. And fuck me awful but those brush tips, it feels like there are just hundreds of them in that thar box and...and...OH NO!"

In the box Chuck bent his long toes forward and pressed the bottoms of his feet against the brush tips he'd just described. A chill of fear and outright apprehension crawled up the young groom's legs, starting at his bare and helpless feet.

"Very good Chuck ol' boy, and those brushes are all hooked up to spindles," the driver laughed, glancing over at Daisy, then at his buddies and then back down at his tied up captive. "Now tell me buddy, what do spindles do exactly?"

"Fucking fucks fucker, I'm no dumb muscle head that you got tied up here, spindles spin...they spin and they rotate and they whirly whirl and they revolve and... FUCK ME!" Chuck gasped out miserably. "Oh no, no, no, don't spin those spindles Mister, whoever the fuck you are...don't spin those spindles with the brushes on them you guys...whoever you guys are that is...you fuckers, you don't know what that'll do to me..."

"Ah but Chuckle my chuckly groom to be, we do know what that'll do to you," the driver laughed again. "It will tickle you...*it will tickle you...*"

That said the van driver pressed a button on the box that Chuck's feet were encased in… A whirring sound was heard as the spindles with the brushes hooked up to them within the box suddenly came to gyrating life.

"OH NO, OH NO, OH GOD DAISY BABY, oh baby, I-I'm a gonna be off an laughin' again darlin', HAHAHA!"

Chuck erupted into loud peals of uncontrollable laughter. "But I sure as hell don't think this is funny at all! HAHAHA! It's true baby, ha, ha, ha, ha! There are brushes in that thar box Daisy, and they's a spinnin' and spinnin' and twirly twirlin' against my poor feets! HAR, HAR, HAR!"

"Stop it, stop it, oh please stop ticklin' him!" Daisy pleaded as Jack squatted down next to her and tweaked one of her nipples as she watched her fiancé laugh his blindfolded head off.

"Looks to me like your intended is really enjoying himself here eh Daisy baby?" Jack laughed. "Yuk, yuk, yuk and yum baby… Sure as all shit, he's all stalked up again in the cock and he just shot a load recently. How about that Daisy baby?"

As Jack spoke he squeezed and jiggled Daisy's nipple through her bikini top, causing her juices to run in her bikini bottom.

"HAHAHA!" Chuck laughed heartily and when the van driver turned a dial on the box the spinning brushes increased in speed.

When he turned another dial the spinning brushes seemed to press harder against Chuck's feet, the bristles of them really digging in. The tickle torture became more maddening with each passing second it seemed.

"D-Daisy, you all gots to do something girl!" Chuck bellowed. "HAW, HAW, HAW! They, they's a gonna kill me with ticklish laughter here!"

"Sorry to say Chuck but your pretty fiancé is a tad tied up at the moment," Adam giggled and squeezed one of Chuck's erect nipples, loving the rubbery hardness of it between his fingertips.

As Chuck laughed and ranted at whoever the fucking fuck it was tweaking his jutted up nipple to leave his damned tit alone still more pre cum oozed from his towering and erect cock.

"AHHHHHHHHHH, ha, ha, ha, ha! Chuck chortled. "Dang it all Daisy, I'm a feelin' all hot and nasty in the cock and balls area! And that amazes me sweetie pie, seein' as I was made to shoot my load so recently and all. I swear to you, I'm a feelin' as if I was duped into eatin' a danged Viagra or somethin' thar of..."

The six men laughed meanly at Chuck's summation of his erect situation...

"Oh Chuck, I'm sorry, I'm a so sorry..." Daisy cried.

"AHHHHHHHHH, Ha, ha, ha, ha, WHOOOO!" was all Chuck could say at that point as the brushes tickled his feet faster yet.

When the spinning brushes connected with his wide arches Chuck saw bright lights and flashing stars behind his blindfold... His feet seemed to spasm inside the box and as they trembled the box shook a bit atop the table, so powerful were the tickled guy's gyrations.

After a good half hour of non stop tickle torture with his feet trapped in the box Chuck's six captors decided to move the "Beth rowed" young man into a new position atop the table...although his feet remained locked in the box as he laughed and laughed and laughed...

Chris and Adam hoisted Chuck's muscular legs upward by his shapely calves as the driver of the van and Sam held the box balanced around the tied down guy's feet.

"WH-WHAT are you jokers up to now?" Chuck managed to say in his heavy Southern accent. "HAH, HAH, HAH! Oh my lord of lords!"

When the box was aimed directly upwards and at the ceiling Jack and Victor tied a goodly amount of rope around it. They then tossed the slack of the rope upwards and around a ceiling beam. Jack yuk, yuk, yukked and yummed as he climbed up on a ladder and tied the slack of the rope tightly around the ceiling beam, thus keeping chuck's legs pointed upward as a result, the box on his feet and the poor young groom to be laughing his fool head off.

"Speed it up a tad more while you're up there buddy," the van driver called out loudly to Jack, wanting to be heard over Chuck's incessant laughter.

"HAHAHA!" Chuck cackled. "NO, NO, NO, NO, those danged brushes are a spinnin' fast enough you he devil!"

Jack laughed and pressed a button on the box. Chuck suddenly screamed louder yet and chortled his head off. Sweat poured down his blindfolded face and his naked muscular body glistened with it under the binding ropes...

Daisy saw the way the men were looking hungrily at her groom's now exposed and gaping raunchy rosebud of an asshole.

"Oh no, you wouldn't, you guy's wouldn't..." Daisy panted, trying desperately now to get herself untied.

She watched as the guys all reached into a cardboard box and helped themselves to electric toothbrushes and long stiff goose feathers.

"HAHAHA!" Chuck laughed crazily. "WH-WHAT do you mean they wouldn't Daisy girl? HAHAHA, HAHAHA what in the lord's tarnation are they up to now pray tell?"

Chris and Adam took up position at Chuck's sides, right by his erect nipples and ribs...

Jack and Victor positioned themselves by the prized area, namely Chuck's exposed and gaping asshole. The van driver and Sam did the honors of grabbing Chuck's succulent ass cheeks and spread the walls of them as far apart as possible, thus really putting the groom's shit chute on display.

The sound of four electric whirring toothbrushes abruptly came to life...

Chuck lifted his head off the table, looked around in blindfolded darkness and smiled insanely behind his eye covering as he laughed.

"OH MY GAWD," the groom to be bellowed in between laughing. "Daisy girl, I don't need me no three guesses here to know what that sound is! HAHAHA! I do brush my teeth everyday after all. OH NO, NO, please Daisy, do something baby! HAHAHA! Don't let them be a ticklin' me with electric toothbrushes to...HAHAHA! Bad enough what they's done to my poor stinkin' feet in that box they got's 'em in... HAHAHA!"

"Chuck, I cain't do nothin' baby," Daisy cried out pitifully. "They got's me tied too tight to this danged chair..."

"OH MY LORD Daisy, but, they are a gonna tickle me now with electric toothbrushes!" Chuck called out, trying to make her know something she already knew it seemed. "HAR, HAR, HAR, oh dang, and this whole seenario just ain't fair Daisy darlin' not fair at all I say! HAW, HAW, HAW!"

Holding up his goose feather Jack trilled, "Tell him Daisy girl..."

"It ain't just electric toothbrushes they's gonna use on you Chuck, they also got's long stiffy lookin' goose feathers in hand..."

Daisy said and Chuck responded by laughing harder yet, his feet spasming like mad in the box...

"Like I said you bastards, this sure is a shitty thing to do to a poor groom to be," Chuck managed to say before he hee hawed his laughter again...

The groom lay there on the table with his ass now exposed and laughed uncontrollably, trying to brace himself for the new sadistic comedy to come...

"Okay guys, and we're off..." the van driver said as he held Chuck's asshole exposed and ready for tickling...

Daisy watched helplessly...

The Electric Toothbrushes and Goose Feathers...

Chris and Adam pressed the whirling bristles of their electric toothbrushes against Chuck's erect nipples, alternating moving them against his ribs and sides. When they weren't tickling him with the toothbrushes they used the tips of the goose feathers on his nipples, strummed them around his huge male cleavage and then teased his sides and ribs with them. Then it was back to the toothbrushes again... As the van driver and Sam held the tied down man's ass cheeks wide apart Jack and Victor did the honors of tickling his shit chute and ass walls with their electric toothbrushes.

"YAHHHHHHHHHHHHHHH!" Chuck screamed shrilly, his head arched back. "FUCKING FUCKED UP FUCKING FUCKERS, DAISY girl, they, they's a ticklin' my stank hole and my tits here! OH MY POOR STANK HOLE, OH DAISY, how mortifyin' is this I ask... HAHAHA!"

As Chuck laughed he jiggled his raised feet in their box prison as the brushes within it spun and spun, tickling the tar out of his feet... As Jack and Victor tickled Chuck's asshole the poor guy farted a few times, really smelling up the cabin.

"AAAARRRRRRHHHHHHH, HAHAHA!" Chuck laughed, his bearded face now sopped in sweat and all harried looking at this point.

Like Chris and Adam were doing alternating between their electric toothbrushes and the goose feathers, the guys at Chuck's gaping and on display asshole did the same. Every time they slid the tips of their feathers into his crack he thought he would literally fly off the table. Good thing he was tied down eh?

"If you boys don't stop a ticklin' him he'll die there on that table," Daisy pleaded miserably. "You boys will make a widow outa me a-fore I'm a hitched..."

"Oh Daisy dear, I don't think you realize just how very strong your fiancé here really is," the van driver laughed and pressed his fingers against Chuck's ass cheek harder as he held it wide open. "Why do you think I decided on tickling the groom to be rather than the bride to be?"

Daisy's eyes opened wide in real terror as she imagined herself laying there tied up being tickle tortured rather than her poor fiancé as he laughed his head off...

Chris and Adam held their spinning toothbrushes against the very tips of Chuck's nipples as Jack yuk, yuk, yukked and yummed as he slid his whirling toothbrush inside the groom's most private crevice. As his most inner sanctum was tickle fucked and his nipples were buzz-cooked Chuck clenched his teeth and made a sound like "RRRRRRRRRRRRRRRRRRR" in between his constant bouts of uncontrollable laughter. Chris and Adam then ran their electric toothbrushes up and down Chuck's raised legs, reaching upward for his thighs as well and back down again. Then they did the same with their goose feathers and again with the toothbrushes. All the while the other guys tickle tormented his asshole while the box that his feet were in tickled him with the spindled spinning brushes... Anyone nearby the cabin or passing it down by the road would have heard the sound of insane and nearly maniacal laughter of a young man being tickle tortured...a young man who was being given his first pre-wedding present...

"YAAAAARRRRRHHHHHH, HAHAHA!" Chuck roared in laughter now as both his nipples and his asshole were tickle tortured at the same time with the electric toothbrushes, all the while he squiggled his feet helplessly in the raised box. "I'm, I'm a beggin' you guys now, oh for fucks sake, HAHAHA, pl-please stop a ticklin' me! Whoever the hell you guys are... I CAN'T TAKE ANYMORE..."

As Chuck pleaded and laughed he was filled with a sense of woe as he felt Jack's toothbrush buried deep in his asshole. It seemed to be making the fillings in his teeth vibrate as Jack worked the brush in further and further. As Daisy watched Jack wedging his toothbrush in Chuck's asshole she wondered (fleetingly) that if it had been her being tickle tortured if he would have done the same to her poor asshole. Her pussy oozed her female wetness at her (fleeting) thought. Chuck's sense of woe was heightened even more-so when he heard the van driver say, "Chuck ol' laughing man, this is only the warm-up..." Chuck's blindfolded eyes rolled in his head in utter disbelief and Daisy also could not believe what she'd just heard. How much more could her poor fiancé take when it came to being tickle tortured?

Tickling The Groom's Armpits

After what seemed like an eternity of tickle torture the six guys finally stopped. They turned off their electric toothbrushes and stopped feather tickling the trapped young man. When Jack extracted his toothbrush from Chuck's hole the groom to be felt a sense of relief mixed with loneliness in his most private bodily crevice. He managed to hold a fart in check as the van driver and Sam lowered his feet back to the table before extracting them from the box they'd been in all that while. When Chuck's feet were again visible and tied to the table legs Daisy again felt that panging in her heart (and other places) at the sight of her fiancé's huge tootsies. At the moment they were sort of red hued. She surmised that was from all the brushes contained in that box having been used to tickle them with all that time. But his feet, my God, Chuck's feet Daisy thought and swooned.

Until this happened she had never given a second thought to Chuck's feet. Okay, granted she did, like most girlfriends did, buy him socks all the time, but didn't all girls and wives do that for their men? There was some kind of old fashioned tradition in that. She had even talked her groom to be into purchasing a pair of sheer black silk socks to go with his tuxedo for the day of their wedding, Chuck calling them prissy socks when he saw them. But his love for Daisy overrode his feelings of prissiness and he agreed to wear the silky stinkers the day of their wedding. Daisy also complained, like most women did when her boyfriend's feet tended to smell real potent and ripe after having been encased in his socks and sneakers or shoes all day. It seemed that whenever Chuck came to her house after a hard day's work he always took his shoes off before relaxing. His socked feet always had a pungent odor. When Daisy would point this out to the guy he said he didn't (or pretended not to) notice the smell whatsoever, grinning though as he said it. But except for these usual things she never gave Chuck's huge feet a thought. Now though, now, looking at them all tied up and slightly reddened from having endured being brush tickled in that box she found herself once more totally aroused. At the moment however, she had more pressing issues to deal with, namely, how to convince the guys who had captured them to release her boyfriend and stop tickling the shit out of him.

"Get him some more water, cool him down a bit," the van driver said. "Let him catch his breath before we get to the next round..."

"The next round?" Chuck garbled. "TARNATION man, don't you think you've done enough to me?"

"Like I said Chuckles, we're just warming up here..." the driver replied meanly.

Chuck tried to think who it was that always called him that, "Chuckles..." But being in the predicament he was in at that moment he could not think all that coherently. He felt a bottle tip pressed to his trembling lips. Gratefully, but foolishly at the same time he sipped down the cool mineral water. He scoffed it down thinking only of slaking his thirst, not knowing that like earlier when he drank the water it was laced with a crushed up Viagra tablet. As he drank and drank his cock seemed to stalk up all the more between his legs...

"His armpits are up for grabs next Daisy girl," Jack said softly to the tied up bride to be. "Yuk, yuk, yuk and yum, but we are gonna toothbrush the shit out of his smelly pits..."

"You boys are monsters, that's what you all are, monsters," Daisy said to Jack as he rubbed her pussy through her bikini.

"You're all wet and soggy here Daisy, looks to me like you're really enjoyin' the show," Jack teased her and glanced over at her beau as he finished drinking the Viagra laced water. "Yuk, yuk, yuk and yum..."

"You keep your hands offen me..." Daisy sneered.

When Chuck was done drinking the water his cock stood up straighter than earlier. Laying there tied down the way he was with his cock sticking straight up and totally erect made for a real nice pretty picture Daisy thought, but quickly pushed the thought away. She couldn't help herself though as she stared at her fiancé's stalked up cock as it dribbled beads of piss and big juicy dollops of pre cum...

"Aw dang Daisy, I-I gets the feelin' I been tricked here when it comes to that thar water baby," Chuck grunted throatily.

"Wh-what do you mean Chuck?" Daisy asked, watching as Adam stepped over to the shelf where the "jar" was.

"I-I'm a realizin' here that each time I drank that water I got all a tingly in the cock and my balls started a churnin' baby," Chuck drawled, sounding like a man balanced perilously on the edge of a sexual precipice. "Just like right now baby, baby. Right after I drank that thar danged water I started a feelin' real sleazy and ornery in the crotch. I-I thinks I been givin' some kind of aphrodeesiac Daisy... I mean, you ain't blindfolded like me darlin'. Just look how my piece of meaty pride is all a stacked up like. I doubt I got that way just from a bein' tickle tortured you know?"

All six of Chuck's captors laughed softly as Daisy said, "I know Chuck, I know..."

A few scant seconds later Chuck grunted loudly and his breath caught in his throat as Adam took his cock again in hand...

"AWWWWWWWWW..." Chuck panted as the stroking began again.

"Coming up, part two of filling the jar with your good stuff buddy," Adam laughed as he held Chuck's manhood straight out and aimed at the mouth of the open jar.

"FUCKER man, dang," Chuck seethed and arched his head back as he felt Victor and the van driver squeezing his nipples, twisting them while Chris kissed the bottom of one of his feet, Sam kissed the other and all the while Adam slowly stroked the tied down groom's cock.

Chuck's pre cum again made for a very slimy lubricant as Adam did the deed...

"Yuk, yuk, yuk and yum huh Daisy baby?" Jack teased the bride as he tweaked one of her nipples. "By the time this here event is over that jar will be chock filled with yer fiancé's sperm."

Daisy's eyes filled with tears of rage as she watched Adam jacking her fiancé's huge tube, the van driver and Victor squeezing his nipples and Chris and Sam kissing the bottoms of his equally huge feet. Chuck's tied feet swayed a bit each time they were kissed. Daisy surmised that he seemed to like that. She swore to herself that if they managed to get out of this mess she would kiss her future husband's feet all the time, no matter how funky they smelled...

"AAWWWWWWHHHH fucking fuckers, I'm a gonna shoot my damned load of sticky juices again here..." Chuck gurgled as his head straightened back out atop the table. "All a you teasin' and a workin' me over the way you are this is just too danged much now and, and... OHHHHRRRRRR FFFFUUUUCCCCCKKKKK! S-SORRY Daisy baby!"

Chuck squirmed in his bondage yet again as Adam held his spewing cock aimed at the open jar. Chuck's mess plopped and slopped into the jar, adding to what he'd deposited in there earlier...

The six guys cheered him on, whooped it up and the cabin was filled with the sounds of utter delight. Daisy's river ran in her bikini bottom...

"Okay Daisy baby, now that he's cum again you can bet your dowry, if you gots one that is, that now he's even MORE ticklish and sensiteeve," Jack teased the bride as he got to his feet. "Yuk, yuk, yuk and yum baby, baby..."

"Oh no, no, y'all cain't tickle poor Chuck again..." Daisy pleaded.

"T-tickle me some more?" Chuck prattled breathlessly as the last remnants of his mess were spewed as Adam emptied his balls. "OH DANG IT ALL DAISY... Is that what I thinks I heard?"

A few ball busting moments later the six men were standing at Chuck's sides, right by his very exposed armpits, three of them on either side of him. The way they had Chuck tied to the table with his muscular arms pulled back and over his head, his wrists cinched together and tied off to one of the table legs made the groom's bushy and sweaty armpits the all-time perfect target for what they had in mind next.

"Okay you guys, lets get our groom to be here laughing again,"

Chuck heard the van driver say and then the sound of six electric toothbrushes whirring to spinning life once more filled the cabin.

"OOOOOHHHHH NO, NO, Daisy girl, I'm in a heap a trouble here I thinks baby…" Chuck managed to say but then he was off and laughing his head off yet again. "HAHAHA! OH NO, NO, not my pits too you guys!"

"Good dental hygiene is most important Chuck ol' Chuckles," the van driver said and whirled his electric toothbrush around and against the side of one of the laughing man's armpits, sending ticklish chills through him.

"HAH, HAH, HAH!" Chuck cackled hyena-like.

He balled his tied up hands into a big fist and yanked and pulled at the ropes, trying desperately to pull free as he laughed.

"Good dental hygiene my raunchy asshole," Chuck prattled angrily. "Nothin' about dental hygiene here, HAHAHA!"

As they strummed and plunked their electric toothbrushes in and around the groom's bushy armpits the six men also took turns squeezing his jutted up nipples. Every time they squeezed his nipples it seemed to make his hardening cock twitch in the wind.

"HAR, HAR, HAR,HAR, HAR, HAR!" Chuck screamed.

Daisy watched helplessly and in tears as her beau, the man she loved, her fiancé was methodically and sadistically tickled… When the van driver looked over at her and winked he directed her attention to the next device that would be used to tickle Chuck. She gasped when she saw the electric shoe-shine machine…

The Electric Shoeshine Machine…

After a good (bad?) half hour of tickle torturing Chuck's randy armpits with the electric toothbrushes the groom to be was a sodden mess atop the table. He willingly gulped down more Viagra laced mineral water and as he did so his cock pounded long, beefy and rigidly hard between his legs.

"OH man, oh Daisy, how much more o' this can I take?" Chuck asked his tied up fiancé when he was done gulping down the water. "My cock is a feelin' all funny again baby, just like when I last drank me the water they all fed me…"

"Don't worry Chuck, as soon as we're done tickling you again I'll pump your slop into the jar for you," Adam said laughingly.

"Okay you guys, its time now for the next device, as I say, that's up for grabs," the van driver said and pointed at Chuck. "Let's get him up off that table and seated in a chair…"

Chuck exhausted from all the constant belly laughing he had done and feeling totally beat to shit did not even resist as he was untied from the tabletop. The van driver and Jack grabbed the groom's arms and yanked him to a seated position atop the table.

"Feeling good there Chuck ol' Chuckles?" Jack asked him. "Yuk, yuk, yuk and yum…"

"What's up with that thar crap man?" Chuck gurgled as he was yanked off the table and to his bare feet. "What is that thar supposed to mean, yuk, yuk, yuk and yum pray tell?"

Jack simply laughed and held tight to the groom's arm as he and the driver moved him to a straight back chair facing Daisy, a few feet away from where she was seated.

"Oh man, this is going to be one for the tickle history books," Adam said as he re-positioned his video camera in Chuck's direction at his new spot.

While Adam got the video camera ready the other men got their tickle captive roped tight to the chair, his arms pulled behind him and his hands roped at the wrists, leaving his feet untied... Daisy watched miserably as Jack did the honors of setting up the electric shoe shine machine in front of Chuck's bare feet while the van driver and Sam rolled a pair of thick and thin black sheer calf length socks onto Chuck's big feet. The socks were a favorite style and color of the guy named Chris, who had brought them along just for the occasion of tickling the groom to be. Adam snickered behind his video camera as he filmed the guys putting the sheer socks on Chuck's feet...

"WH-what are they doin' Daisy?" Chuck barked angrily. "Talk to me here girl. Your poor guy is in one hell of a pickle...Dang it all you guys, puttin' silky feelin' socks of some kind on my big ol' sweaty feet? What's the point of that? Daisy, what in tarnation is goin' on here?"

The van driver looked quickly over at Daisy and put a finger over his lips...

"I don't rightly think they want me a sayin' right now Chuck," Daisy said, sounding sorrow-filled.

"They don't want you a sayin' baby?" Chuck snarled. "And what kind of shit is that pray tell here? They's the ones that have kidnapped you and me baby. And shit, I's the one they tickled and teased and jacked off into a jar. So whatever the fucking fucks you want to say that you feel you want to say Daisy girl you just go on ahead and..."

As Chuck prattled on and on the van driver whipped the blindfold off him. Chuck quickly looked around the large cabin, saw that his captors had all donned their ski masks again and then he looked down to where his tied up fiancé was looking. He followed Daisy's eyes down to the front of his chair he was bound to and he saw besides the socks they'd slid onto his feet...

"HOLY FUCKING SHIT and tarnation again baby," Chuck said as

he took in the sight of his tied up fiancé. "Daisy girl, I've seen those things in electronic magazines and such... That thar is a goddamned high powered, high spinning shoe shining machine. All those fancy shmancy Wall Street dudes that I mentioned earlier has gots one in their offices..."

Looking down at the usual everyday device Chuck did not need three guesses to know how the van driver and his buddies planned to use it on him. As he continued looking down at the machine as it seemed to mock him the groom to be really took in the sight of the damned thing. He wiggled his toes under the sheer thick and thin socks the guys had rolled onto his feet. Dang it all he thought, but they sure as shit looked like the prissy "Wedding socks" that Daisy and the sales guy at the tuxedo place had hoodwinked him into buying just recently. But more-so than the socks he was now wearing it was the machine set up in front of his socked feet that seemed to truly demand his attention. It was a conventional shoe shine machine, the ones with the highly polished chrome bodies. Chuck was able to see his beleaguered naked tied up image in the shiny chrome of the thing. His cock was sticking up and throbbing as he looked past it and down at the next device that would surely be used to tickle torture him...or to be more precise to tickle torture his feet, or to be even more precise, to tickle torture his now socked feet, his sheer socked feet. On either side of the chrome body was a big fuzzy/fluffy cone, one red and one black. The big end of each of the fluffy/fuzzy polishing cones was near the chrome body and each tapered down to a point at both ends. But unfamiliar to Chuck and something he never saw in any electronic magazine or catalogue was where the shoe shine machine's were concerned was that in the top of this one he saw two hatches with handles on each of them. The poor tied up guy had to wonder what those were for... He looked up at his ski masked hosts but did not need to ask them to explain the strange looking contraption to him. Somehow he knew it would all be explained very soon. He looked up at the van driver with his mouth gaping and wide open.

"Who are you guys?" Chuck asked and then looked over

at Daisy. "You've seen their faces haven't you baby? While I was blindfolded you saw their faces I'm sure. They had to put back their ski masks so is I wouldn't see their faces while they let me see this here danged machine at my prissy socked feet! Tell me if you know who they are Daisy girl..."

The van driver held up a finger and wagged it in a "NO" fashion from side to side. Daisy knew that if she told her fiancé would spend more time being tickle tortured, that was for sure. She pursed her lips together and looked helplessly at her intended. The van driver tapped Chuck on his shoulder and directed his attention back to the shoeshine machine at his feet.

"It's, it's a goddamned high speed executive shoeshine machine!" Chuck repeated and his cock twitched as he said those words, those awful words. "Lord is me; I'm a sittin' here all tied and naked in front of my fiancé and six strangers..."

Chuck's cock lurched again and clear pre cum leaked from his wide sexy slit, which trickled down the domed head and then down along the veined sides of his shaft. He saw the way his fiancé looked hungrily at his pre cum oozing cock and then down at his huge socked feet. Even he had to admit that there was something real sexy and vulnerable about the way his huge ol' feet looked in those sheer stinkers his captives had put on him.

"It, it's a fucking shoe shine machine," Chuck said again.

"HA, HA, and yuk, yuk, yuk and yum for you buddy," the van driver laughed, glancing over at Jack as he used the man's strange line. "That is exactly what it is, a very high speedy executive shoe shining machine. But Chuck ol' Chuckles, it looks to us like you've gone and a lost your shoes, or so it would appear, ha, ha, and yuk, yuk, yuk and yum again for you buddy boy. So in place of your shoes we've donned your big stinky feet in special weddin' style socks...just to keep the tradition for your and Daisy's up and comin' nuptials..."

"FUCK me, you guys, whoever the fucks you all are, you all are really enjoyin' all this aren't yous?" Chuck asked the men miserably as they all stood watching his torments; his head lolling back as he looked helplessly up at the van driver.

It was this man who seemed to be in total control of the entire situation Chuck surmised. But if Daisy knew who he and the others were why oh why didn't she speak her mind the groom to be had to wonder.

"Chuckles ol' boy, me and my buddies here want you to benefit totally from this machine by having your shoes, well, in your case your sexy wedding socks polished," the driver snickered. "This machine is one of your weddin' presents after all."

"Th-that's real nice man, whoever the fuck you may be, b-but you cain't polish socks," Chuck whimpered. "Fuck man and dang, iffen you put that thing on it will, it'll, oh God, I hates to even says it, but I'll says it anyways here, it'll tickle my damned feet. OH FUCK MISTER, it will tickle my prissy socked feet, not polish my socked feet! There is a difference you cad! (Chuck was nearly crying now.) There's a fucking difference here and you all knows it!"

As chuck spoke and pleaded his balls actually shifted in their sac and his cock bounced long and hard more and more. Fuck, it actually felt to the groom to be that his poor balls were changing positions and rolling around in his sac. Or perhaps that was just his nerves causing that sensation?

"Listen man, and the rest of you guys, you cain't do this to me, now come on guys, I'm a groom to be in a few short days and you've done enough to me already," Chuck gurgled, doing his best to try to talk his way out of impending tickle doom. "Come on now, you boys don't know what this will do to me...iffen you does it that is..."

"HA, ha, and yuk, yuk, yuk and yum, but yes we do Chuckles, it will tickle you," the van driver said in a mocking high pitched tone of voice as he then squatted down next to his captured prey. *"It will tickle your pretty sheer socked feet, yuk, yuk, yuk and yum."*

Jack took that as his cue to hunker down on the other side of the tied up sheer socked groom. All the other assembled guys watched intently as the van driver and Jack each took one of Chuck's feet by the ankle and calf. They lifted the groom's socked feet and moved them toward the shoe shine device in front of him.

"Now, like I said Chuckles ol' Chuck, this ordinary shoe shine machine is one o' your and Daisy's weddin' presents, but it sher ain't a conventional model, I'll tell you that," the driver said as he held one of Chuck's feet real tight. "Because you see, me and my buddies here, we added to this high and speedy shoe shiner."

"You, *you added to it?*" Chuck asked. "What are you guys, mad scientist inventors of some sorts?"

"Yes Chuck, we added to it, you see, instead of tickling your silky socked feet from the sides, the way it was originally made to polish shoes, it's a gonna tickle your feets from the inside," the guy explained and as he held one of Chuck's feet in one hand he opened one of the hatches on the device that had been mentioned earlier, the hatches that were on the topmost part of the shoe shining machine.

Chuck looked down again with his mouth hanging open, a feeling of beyond sheer (socked) terror now engulfing him. He saw that there were two very wide openings inside the danged device, big and wide enough for a guy's feet to fit into just perfectly, and in this case it would be the groom's wedding socked feet fitting just perfectly in there. And further down in the device, inside those wide openings Chuck saw to his dismay what looked like hundreds of round, definitely motorized soft shoe cleaning bristles. To further the groom's dismay it appeared that the tips of those bristles were glistening, as if they had been treated with some kind of machine oil.

"Getting the picture now buddy?" the van driver asked and

Chuck suddenly felt his poor feet sweating in the silky black sheer socks, an erotic and musty scent suddenly wafting up to his nostrils.

It was also the scent of sheer (socked) terror that he smelled. His hard cock twitched in fear and became even more erect (what was up with that?) as his poor balls churned with a new mess of gobs upon gobs of pent-up sperm.

"Oh man, no, no, *oh Gawd please no,*" Chuck whimpered. "What is Sam hell do I have to say to get through to you all numb skulls?"

"Now, once your sexy socked tootsies are in there we'll close the hatch, that way you won't be able to pull your feet away from the machine," the van driver laughed as he and Jack gripped Chuck's socked calves tighter now, hefting them up off the floor and moving them over the openings in the shoe shining device.

"Y-you bastards," Chuck said nearly in a whisper that reeked of real terror by then. "What a twisted thing to do to that machine, and to our weddin' present at that. You boys have turned a normal everyday executive device into a fucking *torture device!* And, and, oh man, and not to mention what a twisted and really fucked up thing you're about to do to me! OH GOD YOU ALL, leggo of my feet, *please, leggo of my damned feet...*"

Chuck cringed in the chair, watching as the men ignored him and slid his socked feet into the two holes in the shoe shine device, plunging them in there to be more precise. The groom felt as if his socked feet had been swallowed up. Before he could make a move to yank his feet back out of the device Jack said, "Yuk, yuk, yuk and yum" and closed the hatch around them and he and the van driver slid the latches locked on them, thus trapping Chuck's sweaty socked feet within the shoe shining device.

"Listen man, before you all start tickle torturin' me again, at least tell me this, one of you, please tell me this, what is the point of all this?" Chuck asked miserably, looking down woefully at his poor feet in the device now, only the very tops of his sheer socks showing and somehow the groom to be found that to be sort of comical looking. "Why you guys, why the hell are you tickling me like this?"

"First, because you're about to be married, and all grooms to be deserve an initiation of some sort, and this is yours Chuck ol' Chuckles, plus because you are very, *very* ticklish," the van driver replied and placed his finger on a switch on the device.

Around that switch were inscribed the words "FAST, FASTER, and FASTEST."

"And second, comedy," the driver continued in his reply to Chuck, his finger resting on the control button of the shoe shine device teasing and mocking the groom to be awfully. "You see Chuck we all love comedy and we all just love to hear a guy laugh."

"Comedy? Dog gone comedy?" Chuck ranted, looking down at the guy as he hunkered next to him. "Fucking comedy huh? Look then, I gots an idea here, we can rent a danged movie, a really funny movie, that way we can all laugh. Me and my fiancé wouldn't need to be tied up, just all of us, whoever you boys are, having a fun time and laughing at a funny movie."

Chuck's feet were pressed into and sweating profusely now in that damned shoe shining machine, surrounded all around and at every inch by those bristles, soft but prickly bristles. And from his experience Chuck knew, *he just knew* that those bristles had been treated with some kind of lubricating oil thus that would make them even pricklier. Chuck felt as if those fucking bristles were actually hugging his feet, like as if they were in love with them. He could feel them on the bottoms of his socked feet, against his arches, pressed up against all of his wiggling toes, over both sides of his ankles, on the tops of his feet and even under his heels. He realized with a sickening sense of dread that both of his poor feet were about to go once again to "TICKLE HELL..." As he and the van driver spoke to each other and all the other ski masked men watched the bristles were still, but with that guy's finger on the control switch the groom to be was afraid that that was about to change dramatically. And his cock, God, how the groom's cock was pulsing, he was totally leaking pre cum. Somehow he knew he had been duped into gulping down an aphrodisiac when they'd fed him that water each time. Never before had he felt so sleazy and worked up in the crotch. What had leaked out earlier had dried up and become very sticky and stiff on his cock shaft, but with all the tickling that he had endured it seemed that his poor tortured balls just kept pushing out his clear thick liquid. And it continued to coat his cock head and eventually his thick veined shaft as well. From the way Daisy was looking at his shiny cum slicked cock Chuck could tell that she could not wait for the wedding night. His hard cock had been stimulated, tickled and jacked off into a jar, of all things! At that point Chuck had lost track of time. How long since which ever one of them had jacked him off last? Embarrassed as he was to say it his poor cock ached for contact, for friction, for something, *anything* to make him cum, anything to climax and trigger his two aching balls to once more pump out their massive overstock of sperm that just seemed to be building and building in them...over and over again...even after he'd cum twice already...

"Funny movie, a funny movie," the van driver said laughingly, glancing over at Adam's video camera as it did its dirty work capturing the groom's tickle torments on film. "Yeah, I a suppose we could laugh at a funny movie at that Chuck ol' Chuckles. And pray tell Chuck, what title would you suggest? Take a look over yonder at that video camera buddy. I assure you, there is no movie that has ever been made that anyone would find as funny as this one that we're a makin' here Chuckles. Now tell me, what title would you suggest for the movie you're a starring in? The Laughing Groom to be maybe? Hardy, har, and har buddy boy..."

"And yuk, yuk, yuk and yum," Jack joined in and all the men laughed.

"We all here really enjoy laughing at you while you're laughing so hard Chuck ol' Chuckles," the van driver said.

"Look man, please, I'm a begging you now, I'm a really begging here," Chuck drawled, his voice making panting sounds. "You've all a seen how very ticklish I am. I am really and awfully ticklish guys!"

"Why Chuckles, of course we all a know how ticklish you are," the driver said, grinning sadistically through his ski mask and nodding his head. "That's why we decided to do this to you before your a weddin' day. And I most of all out of all o' the guys here am thoroughly enjoyin' this adventure. And from the way you've been laughing I just knows that you think all of this is soooooo funny...right Chuckles?

As Chuck tried hard to think who it was that always called him Chuckles the van driver laughed one last time and then flipped the switch on the shoe shine device to the "FASTEST" position. Suddenly, the shoe shine machine came to whirring life, looking for shoes to shine and finding none it had no choice but to go to work on Chuck's socked feet. Inside that device all the bristles that had been hugging the groom's socked feet before were now moving beyond rapidly across, over, around and under the tied up guy's sheer socked feet. There was no spot on Chuck's devilishly ticklish feet that was not being tickled and teased by those spinning whirling bristles. It felt to the poor guy like his feet were being vibrated and tickled on by thousands and thousands of tiny nibbling teeth...

"AAAAAAYYYYYYYYYY Ha, ha, ha, haha, oh you bastards, YOU BASTARDS, Ha, ha, ha, ha!" Chuck screamed in laughter. "WH-what a fucking fucked up way to clean a guy's smelly socks! HAR, HAR, HAR!"

Daisy watched and her pussy leaked her female juices...

"AAAAAYYYYYYYYYYYY Ha, ha, ha, haha! C-c'mon man, c'mon you guys," Chuck squealed. "HEE, hee, hee, hee, hee, hee, hee, hee, hee, hee, hee, hee, hee, hee! It, it's a ticklin' and ticklin' my feet here!

SH-shit on shanola you bastards, stop this thing! HAHAHA!"

So there the groom sat bound up good and tight in that straight backed chair, his heavy sperm loaded balls aching. His goddamned cock was poking holes in the air above his lap it seemed and leaking more and more pre cum than the groom would have ever thought possible.

"My Lord, my socked feet are a being shined here," Chuck ranted in between laughing.

"Not exactly buddy boy," Jack laughed. "Your socked feet are a being shined and tickled and tickled and tickled and tickled. Yuk, yuk, yuk and yum!"

The groom looked down and grimaced as he laughed at the sight of his socked feet trapped in a warped version of a shoe shine machine as they were tickled unmercifully. It seemed to him that somehow the sheer socks his captors had rolled onto him along with the combination of the oiled bristles were making the tickling sensations reach new heights. Then, in total hysteria the groom to be suddenly felt something else, something on his feet besides the tickling sensations he was being so meanly subjected to. Besides the tickling sensations all over his feet Chuck suddenly realized that the spinning tickling bristles had started eating those sheer socks off him. To be more precise, the bristles were spinning and tickling his socked feet, but then, suddenly they somehow began eating the socks right off him, *right off his feet.* The spinning motion he supposed was what caused the bristles to start pulling at the ultra-thin socks. Looking down through tear filled laughing eyes Chuck saw the socks begin to stretch and slide down his calves into the bowels of the shoe shine device that his feet were presently trapped in. Not only was the damned machine tickling him, but now it was fixing to get his sheer socks off him and to tickle his bare feet it seemed.

"OH MY LORD, check this out, HAHAHA! TH-the fucking shoe

shiner is a eatin' the danged sheer weddin' socks offen my big ol' feet!" Chuck hyena laughed and at the sight of his socks being chewed off his feet by the machine his captors joined in the folly of his laughter. "Oh my, there they go, another inch Daisy, I'm a losin' my weddin' socks here, HAHAHA!"

Little by little the socks were yanked and pulled down by the spinning bristles. As Chuck laughed and laughed and watched the machine just kept on tickling him and devouring his socks. Chuck's captors laughed and at the sight of his socks being pulled down they pointed at his feet. Now, all the assembled men were laughing along with their tickle captive, but obviously laughing for different reasons. Inch by inch Chuck's socks disappeared into the torturous shoe shining machine. Lower and lower went the sheer socks as the wicked device tickled and tickled his slowly being bared feet. Down went the socks a bit more and then they were gone. Like magic the sheer socks had disappeared from Chuck's feet and went down below the part of the machine that his feet were encased in. The groom to be could not believe it himself the hilarity of what was transpiring. The damned shoe shine machine was eating and stripping the socks that the guy's had rolled onto his feet off him. Chuck could no longer see the socks at that point but he sure as all hell felt the bristles as they attacked his bared flesh that was now uncovered because of the slowly receding socks, which were now over his heels. The tickling became more maddening as the sock stripping went on. Chuck felt the socks inch toward his wiggling toes then they were at his toes and then, then they were gone, eaten right off his poor feet and gulped down into the bowels of the shoe shine machine.

"OH MY, oh Daisy, fuck me dreadful baby," Chuck cackled. "HAHAHA, HAHAHA, th-that fucking shoe shine device from hell just stripped me of those socks baby! Did you a see that?" "I saw Chuck, I saw," Daisy replied, trying her best to stifle her own laughter.

Chuck's captors found it to have been hilarious. The groom

to be simply found it to be just one more humiliation, and awful of all awfuls the tickling went on and on and on. Now the bristles in the shoe shine device were able to get directly to Chuck's hot sweaty naked feet.

"AAAYYYYYRRRR, HAHAHA fuck, this sure as hell is givin' new meanin' to the word "tickle!" Chuck crowed. Y-you all are a drivin' me crazy here! Ha, ha, ha, ha, m-my socks are a gone but it's still a tickling my feet, stop, stop, stop this thing, ha, ha, ha, ha! Whoever you guys are…"

Chuck continued laughing crazily and witlessly even long after the black sheer socks were gone.

"Y-you guys, holy fucking shit you guys, ha, ha, ha, ha!" Chuck screamed. "Did you guys a see that? DID you fuckin' see that? HAR, HAR, HAR, ohhhhhhh God, y-your devilish machine ate those a socks right off my tickly feet! Ha, ha, ha, ha!

"Of course we saw it, that was hysterical buddy boy," the van driver laughed and squatted down behind the tickle captive as he sat tied to the straight back chair.

The fast spinning bristles in the machine massaged and lapped hungrily at Chuck's bare smelly feet. To the groom to be they felt like a thousand and more tiny teeth, nibbling at his feet as they tickle tormented every last part of his poor feet. To Chuck all of this felt kind of monotonous at that point. How much more would they tickle him? Who the hell were they? Would he and Daisy make it to their wedding day? Chuck wondered these things as he laughed and laughed.

"OH GAWD Daisy, I cain't a help all this here laughing I'm a doin' baby, ha, ha, ha, ha!" Chuck chortled helplessly. "I'm just a poor sap of a guy laughing his head off and a relating all this laughter to you. This is these guy's fault baby, the ones that a kidnapped our asses! And you know what's really funny Daisy baby? HAHAHA, you know what is really so danged funny?"

"Wh-what's that Chuck?" Daisy asked.

"I-I don't think that all this here laughter that's bein' forcefully extracted from me is so funny at all baby, HAHAHA!" Chuck laughed in response. "I'm a finding out the hard way here that laughing and funny do not necessarily go together baby! HAHAHA, I'm not a laughin' here a cause I'm havin' fun baby, I'm a chortlin' and cacklin' because of this goddamned machine that my feet is trapped in! HAHAHA!"

"I know Chuck, I know..." Daisy said sorrowfully.

"I mean, it sure was funny to watch those socks get eaten right offen my feets huh?" Chuck prattled on laughingly. "HAHAHA, I'm sure that iffen I wasn't on the receivin' end of all this I would have laughed my head off too seeing some guy get his prissy socks eaten off his trapped feet by some danged machine! HAHAHA! But to me, the poor sap that's it a all bein' done to, Daisy, to me, it sure ain't funny! I'm mean, I'm naked here baby, naked in front a you and these total strangers! HAHAHA!"

At that point in his tirade Chuck looked up at Jack and screamed, "S-so much for shining up stinky socks huh? HAHAHA!"

"Yuk, yuk, yuk, and yum," Jack responded.

From behind him the van driver grabbed Chuck's upper arms real tight; right above where the rope was lashed snugly over and over the tickle captive's huge biceps. The guy hoisted Chuck a few inches off the chair so that now Chuck's sweaty balls swung back and forth a few times and the rope over his upper torso rubbed against the groom's very big, fleshy nipples.

"Oh dang it all man, you really know how to play me Mister," Chuck drawled as his heavy balls swung and his nipples were massaged by the ropes.

The van driver did just that, he played his tickle captive like he was a musical instrument that needed some fine tuning. Chuck's naked feet now felt like they had thousands upon thousands of feathers brushing every square inch of the skin on them. Another monstrous way to describe it was that it felt like thousands of ants crawling all around and over his bare feet from his heels and ankles all the way to his ticklish toes, which, just for the record were wiggling like they had never wiggled before. Of course the groom to be could not see his toes at that moment being that they were locked in the annals of the machine, but he sure could feel the involuntary wiggling they were doing down in there as the bristles kissed them all over and in between each toe as well.

"OHHHHHHHHH, ha, ha, ha, haH-hey, whoever you are, leggo of me man, and turn, ha, ha, ha, ha, and turn, HAW, HAW, HAW, turn off this FUCKING machine!" Chuck screamed through uncontrollable fits of laughter as the guy seemed to be adjusting him in the chair.

Chuck's poor heavy hanging balls swung back and forth and his cock, hard as a rock and once more stalked up and oozing pre cum pointed at the ceiling. Screaming loud laughter escaped the groom to be, along with frothy spittle as it spewed from his mouth. As he looked upward Chuck did not take notice of the rest of the guys as they all helped themselves to long stiff goose feathers that Jack had had stashed in a backpack. The tied up groom was still babbling, laughing, begging to be released as the van driver hoisted him upwards in the chair as much as the ropes would allow. As Chuck laughed, as sweat poured off him, as he looked up at the ceiling he did not have an iota of a clue as to what the fucking fuck the van driver and his buddies were up to now. Actually, Chuck was too busy laughing to give a rat's ass what they were up to now, as he would have so aptly stated, had he been able to. Chuck's utmost concern at that moment was for his being tickle tortured naked feet and he wondered how much more of this he would be forced to endure. Suddenly, he heard Daisy holler, "No, no, don't do that to him!" and all at once Chuck felt something new, almost like he had just sat on a goddamned branding iron or something.

"MY BALLS! OH Gods, not my balls you fuckers," Chuck ranted, looking down again and seeing that the guys were all using their goose feathers to tickle his balls with while the van driver held him aloft on the chair. "EEEEEEEYOWWWWWWWWW! Ha, ha, ha, ha! Oh my Lord of Lords you guys, what, what, what, ha, ha, ha, ha, what the fuck are you doing to me now? You blowhards are makin' me crazy here!"

The guys all spun and twirled their feathers against, around and all over Chuck's cum engorged gonads and it looked as if his poor balls were actually jumping in their sac like Mexican jumping beans. His ball sac bubbled up in goose flesh; the guys were relentless as they tickled the groom's balls all the more. His balls drew up tight with big sexy bumps sprouting on his scrotum where the hair follicles were. But alas, they could not draw themselves away from those feathers, those guys whipping and tickling feathers. This was an all new torment for the groom to be because although his cock shaft was not being touched it was simply pumping hard and stiff in the air, trying desperately to find some relief. And to his disbelief the way he was being tickled on the feet and balls was causing him to ooze more and more pre cum in buckets it seemed. Chuck felt as if he was being tickled to death at his feet and balls and at the same time he was being sexually teased and stimulated beyond belief with no relief. Gawd, he thought, but these guys who had captured him and Daisy sure had evil minds. He looked at his captors through huge laugh caused tears and as he laughed himself silly the guys all grinned at him through their ski masks. They were obviously enjoying every scant second of all this...

After a long while later Chuck realized he was still laughing, even though the shoe shining machine and the guys tickling him with their feathers had all stopped. Somehow the groom to be had lost track of time and his sense and by then his cock was incurably hard, begging, pleading for relief by then. When the tied up groom to be realized that the machine his feet was in had been turned off he felt really stupid because he was still laughing. He managed to stop laughing and took a few even breaths and gulps of air. After he was again able to breathe somewhat normally he looked up at the van driver through hazy vision...

"Th-thank you man, oh God, thank you, ha, ha, ha, ha" Chuck said, a few laughs still escaping him. "Oh for the love of God and his angels you blasted mugs tickled my danged balls..."

"Uh yeah, we did at that Chuckles, even you have to admit that that was funny," the van driver said and as the other guys gathered around Chuck he again squatted down next to the shoe shining machine.

"Yeah, a real barrel of laughs, hardy fucking har, but I'm the poor fuck in the barrel you bastards," Chuck drawled, looking up and around at his ski masked captors as the van driver opened the hatch of the shoe shining machine.

Before the guy could grab at Chuck's feet to extract them from the machine the groom to be pulled them out on his own accord, not that he would be able to escape from the six men, seeing as he was tied to the chair. But, for whatever the reason it gave Chuck a small sense of freedom to be able to remove his own feet from the clutches of that infernal device. Looking down Chuck saw that his feet were red and shiny looking all over...

"Oh God..." he whispered.

Chuckling sadistically, the van driver, who it appeared, was the ringleader in this entire scene being played out, reached into the shoe shine device. Laughing meanly along with his five cohorts he held up the black silk socks. They were all mangled, twisted and moist looking, but still intact. The machine hadn't ripped them at all. Chuck watched and his hard cock twitched as the van driver held the stinking socks to his visible nose and mouth and said, "Whew, your feet really are all sweaty and randy buddy. We just put these stinkers on you and they smell like you've had them on all day. So tell me Chuckles, do you want these socks back on your feet again for the next tickle device?" The groom's heart sank like the Titanic at just the very thought of yet another tickle device...or, to be more precise, another device of torture.

"Man that sure was something though huh Chuckles, huh guys?" the driver asked, still laughing and still holding the sheer socks in hand. "The way that machine ate your socks right off your feet buddy? As you would say, fucking fucks, I didn't expect that to happen."

"FUCKER, fucking fucks is right man!" Chuck suddenly thundered having lost most of his patience at that point it would appear. "I didn't expect any of this to happen today! What the fucking fucks is this after all? A guy is out having a nice date with his fiancé and he winds up kidnapped and tickle tortured?" As Chuck ranted madly, letting off all his steam the van driver laughed and rolled the sheer socks back onto the tickle captive's feet. He then grabbed Chuck by his calves.

"H-HEY man, what are you a doin'?" Chuck screeched at the guy. "Look, I'm sorry I yelled okay? I'm really sorry. Just don't... don't..."

"You know Chuck, it was, it really was so damned funny the way that machine ate these socks off your feet that I thought we would give it another good go," the van driver said and began sliding Chuck's poor, again socked feet into the wide open holes of the shoe shining device.

"OH GOD NO, NOT AGAIN, please!" Chuck squealed and then the guy closed the hatch, locking the groom's feet in again. "FUCKER!" "Yuk, yuk, yuk and yum," Jack laughed. "Looks like that machine is hungry for weddin' socks eh Chuckles?"

The van driver wasted no time. He turned the machine on for the second go round and once again Chuck's socked feet were being brutally tickle tortured. All the guys laughed meanly at the guy's plight, as Daisy watched miserably yet somehow enticed as her groom's socks were again being eaten from his being tickled feet. And just for the hell of it all the guys once again took up their feathers and took turns tickling Chuck's bulging balls. So, as the guy's feet were tickled in the shoe shine device for the second time and as his sheer socks were slowly eaten from his feet by said device his balls were again tickle tortured relentlessly again as well.

"Ha, ha, ha, ha, AAAAAAHHHRRRRR!" Chuck screamed his laughter again. "Daisy, LOOKIT this hyar shit baby, m-my socks, they, they're a disappearin' again! And, and what good hosts we gots here baby, ha, ha, ha, ha, to make sure that my sweaty balls don't miss out on the fun too!"

All Daisy could do was look helplessly at her fiancé as he chortled and choked and laughed as he spoke.

"You are going to be amazed at what we have planned for you next buddy boy," the van driver said directly into Chuck's ear as the groom laughed and laughed...and laughed and laughed...and laughed and laughed...

A good half hour or so later Chuck was again lying atop the table, tied down and blindfolded as he had been before his captors had subjected him to the shoe shine machine. As soon as Chuck was again blindfolded all six of the guys took off their ski masks. Chuck's feet were again bare, the socks having been left in the shoe shine device this time after they had been eaten off him.

"OOOOOOOOHHHH," Chuck groaned in a man's passion as Adam once more did his chore of stroking the groom's gargantuan cock.

Adam held Chuck's pulsing man meat straight out and his piss hole aimed at the open jar that already contained two of the groom's shots of cum.

"OHHHHRRRR GAWD, fucker, whoever you are, jackin' and a yackin' my cock again," Chuck panted. "I think I mighta mentioned it to you guys already, but I'll say it again just in case here, I ain't no faggot! Get your hands offen my danged baby maker you joker!"

"But Chuckles, like I told you man, after you laugh your head off into oblivion after we tickle torture you I'm a gonna milk you," Adam laughed, imitating Chuck in the way he spoke.

Chuck's sweaty and tingling balls bounced up and down real sexily in their sac as Adam stroked and choked the groom's pre cum slicked shaft. While Adam was busy pulling Chuck's pud the van driver and Jack were getting Daisy untied from the chair.

"Now Daisy baby, as a weddin' present for you we gots a real treat in store here," the van driver said softly as he and Jack grabbed her scrawny arms, hefting her out of the chair and to her feet.

"WH-what in tarnation are you boys up to now?" Daisy asked as she was brought to her feet, watching at the same time as her man was jacked off, her pussy watering at the sight of that.

"Yuk, yuk, yuk and yum," Jack said laughingly. "You all will find out soons enough Daisy honey, honey."

"OHHHHRRRRRR FUCKING fuck fucker," Chuck growled a few seconds later and then all the guys and Daisy watched as yet another good mess of the groom's slop was siphoned from him and sloshed in the jar by Adam. "OOHHHRRRRRRR, you guys keep this up and I won't have any left for the weddin' night..."

As soon as Chuck was done spewing his load Adam capped the jar tight, placed it back up on the shelf and re positioned his video camera as the van driver and Jack brought Daisy over to the table that her groom was tied to. The six men quickly donned their ski masks again and Chris took Chuck's blindfold off him.

"Looks like you get to watch the next event oh groom to be," Jack chuckled and squeezed one of Chuck's nipples real hard, twisting it for good measure. "Yuk, yuk, yuk, and yum."

Watching Jack tweak her fiancé's nipple sent ripples through Daisy's being. Chuck let his eyes once more adjust to the light and then he looked up to see his poor fiancé in the van driver and Jack's clutches.

"Now Daisy, sweet thang, how is this for a weddin' buffet?" the van driver asked the bride to be, positioning Daisy by Chuck's tied up bare feet.

Daisy secretly longed for her man's feet. Looking down at them all sweaty, glistening from the tickling they'd endured, smelly and all tied up her mouth watered. At that moment she didn't know that relief was just a few licks away.

"A live groom to be cocktail hour Daisy baby," the van driver said as Jack tied Daisy's hands back behind her. "At the weddin' the bride and groom feed each other a piece of cake, its tradition honey. "But here today we's a startin' a new tradition..."

"Yeah, you is gonna feast on your groom to be's stinky feet," Jack laughed. "Yuk, yuk, yuk and YUM for you Daisy..."

"What in the fucking fuck did I just hear here?" Chuck snarled. "I ain't a danged buffet for anybody to be a feastin' on let alone my poor kidnapped fiancé! Fucking rascals you boys are! WHOOOOOOO! HAHAHA!"

To stop Chuck's prattle Sam trailed a fingertip up and down the bottom of one of Chuck's naked feet.

"Okay Daisy baby, here's the new tradition I just mentioned to y'all," the van driver said, moving the young lady closer to Chuck's tied up feet at the end of the table he lay on. "Like most grooms to be I'm sure Chuckles here has cold feet. Now, we warmed 'em up a tad by ticklin' and shoe shinin' them, as you seen already. But now it's your turn to warm up those feet of his. Go on Daisy baby; give your husband to be a nice weddin' present."

The driver let go of Daisy's arms and left her standing there with her hands tied behind her at her man's tied up feet.

"Oh Chuck, *oh Chuck,*" Daisy said with tears in her eyes. "I-I really don't, I don't want to tickle you baby, but your feet...Oh Chuck, your feet, they, they's a beautiful baby..."

All the men in the room stifled their laughter and Adam's video camera captured the magic moment as the expression on Chuck's face became one of utter disbelief.

"Daisy, what in tarnation is you talking about girl?" Chuck ranted through clenched teeth. "Are you joinin' their ranks baby, baby? You suddenly got a thang for my feets too Daisy girl?"

Without another word Daisy leaned down and began by one kissing her man's toes.

"HUHHHHHHH! Holy fucks and land o goshin Daisy girl, you is kissin' my danged toes, and I gots to say that that feels great baby, baby!"

Daisy nodded "Yes" and followed up the toe kissing by sucking two of Chuck's small toes into her mouth and swirled her tongue on them.

"OOOOOO, ha, ha, ha, ha, that a tickles baby, that a tickles at that," Chuck squawked. "Iffen you love me baby don't tickle me..."

With her hands tied behind her Daisy leaned down a bit further and began kissing the bottoms of her man's beefy feet, pressing her lips and tongue against the soles, inhaling her rugged fiancé's raw foot scent.

"MMMMMM..." Daisy swooned.

Then, she stuck her tongue out and without wanting to, but not able to stop herself it seemed she began flicking the tip of her tongue up and down and up and down the bottoms of Chuck's feet.

"YAHHHHHHHHHH, ha, ha, ha, ha!" Chuck screamed and was off and laughing yet again. "Daisy, you is what would be called a traitor girl! OH MY FUCKS, you is ticklin' my danged feet Daisy!" "I love you Chuck, and I love your feets as well," Daisy said and quickly resumed lick tickling her fiancé's feet.

The six ski masked men joined in Chuck's laughter as he whooped it up atop the table, struggling madly in the bondage as his fiancé licked his feet like a woman possessed.

"Looks like we turned them thar tables on you eh Chuck ol' Chuckles?" the van driver sneered.

Daisy's tongue felt like it was moving at hundreds of miles per hour as she licked and kissed and slathered it over and over Chuck's arches now, they being the most tickle sensitive spots on his big feet.

"AAAAAHHHHHHH HAHAHA!" Chuck laughed screamingly. "WH-what are you doin' to me here girl? Oh my lord of lords, you guys have a brainwashed my poor fiancé here! HAHAHA! Daisy, Daisy, please stop, stop it baby, baby! HAHAHA! EEEEEEEEEEEEEEEEEEEEEE EEE! HAW, HAW, HAW, oh my fucks, oh my shit, but this is downrights evil!"

Daisy hunkered herself upward and slid her tongue next over the thickly veined tops of Chuck's feet. As she licked the thick skin Chuck's toes twitched back and forth. Watching his fiancé lick tickle his feet somehow caused his Viagra induced erection to stalk up even more. Daisy looked at Chuck's erection with her tongue hanging out, but instead of going for the gusto she licked his feet some more...

When she licked Chuck's heels the groom to be arched his head back, looked behind him at his captors and the room spun as he laughed and laughed and laughed and laughed...

"HAHAHA! D-Daisy baby, I still loves you girl, but I sure as all hell and heaven wish you would stop a ticklin' my danged feets!" Chuck pleaded.

As Daisy lick tickled her fiancé's feet Sam and Victor joined in the fun by tickling Chuck's ribs and sides while the van driver and Jack went to work on his sweaty armpits.

"YAAAAHHHHHHHHHHHH! I really am the danged tickle buffet here!" Chuck laughed and then all he heard was the sound of a man laughing nearly insanely as his head seemed to revolve in a revere orbit of sorts.

A while later Chuck was blindfolded again, all the men had taken off their ski masks and as Jack quickly retied Daisy to her chair the van driver fed Chuck some Viagra laced cool mineral water.

"There you go buddy boy, down the hatch," the van driver said as Chuck chugged the cool liquid down, his Adam's apple bobbing sexily.

Chuck's huge stalk pointed up at the ceiling between his legs, his once more cum chocked balls resting on the tabletop as he gulped the water. His cock twitched back and forth, it oozed thick droplets of pre cum and Daisy's mouth salivated at the sight of that. While she had been licking his feet she had considered gobbling his huge erection into her mouth and pleasuring him a bit. God knew, after what the six guys had done to him tickle-wise Chuck sure as hell did deserve some pleasuring. But somehow Daisy got the feeling that had she attempted to pleasure her fiancé in that way the van driver would not have allowed it. For some reason the men wanted her man's slop collected in that danged jar.

"I-I gots to pee," Chuck drawled, sounding very Forrest Gump when he was done drinking the water.

"Not a problem buddy o' mine," Adam said, sounding evil. "We have one more tickling stint to put you through and then after I milk you in the jar again I'll use another jar for your yellow stream…"

Chuck pursed his lips together, his balls churned and he mumbled miserably, "Oh dang it all, theys a gonna tickle me yit again…"

Then, a few moments later Daisy watched as the van driver produced a jar of skin cream of some sort. He and Jack slathered her fiancé's feet liberally with the cream, making sure to really spread the stuff well and all over her tied down groom's tootsies.

"Dang, what now, feels like I'm getting a goddamned pedicure here," Chuck ranted through clenched teeth.

"Close, but no cigar for the groom to be," Jack chuckled. "Yuk, yuk, yuk and yum…"

"Pedicures is for women folk," Chuck seethed as his feet were sopped and slathered with the skin cream.

When the van driver and Jack were done Chris and Adam next took their turn. They rubbed the cream between and all over Chuck's toes, meanly stealing tickle moments as they did so.

"Ho, ho, ho, I don't think I needs no three guesses here to know what you mugs are up to now," Chuck panted as his bare feet were soaked in skin cream.

"Figured it out already eh Chuck ol' Chuckles?" the van driver asked. "That skin cream is going to make those huge feets of yours even more tickle sensitized buddy... HO, ho, ho for you..."

When Chuck's feet were drenched and sopping with skin cream Sam and Victor each took a portable, battery operated hairdryer out of a box. They stepped to Chuck's creamy looking feet and aimed their driers at them. They clicked them on to a "High Heat" setting and began blow drying the groom to be's slicked feet.

"H-hey, what now?" Chuck ranted, straining at his bonds. "F-fucking fuckers, what in tarnations are you mugs up to now? Daisy, are they a blow dryin' my danged creamed up feets heeyar?"

"Th-that's what they're a doin' Chuck, although I don't knows why," Daisy responded.

"Allow me to explain you two lovebirds," the van driver said, stepping next to Chuck and tweaking one of his jutted up nipples.

Chuck's huge hard cock twitched and dribbled pre cum as his nipple was squeezed.

"When you cream up a tickle victim's feet and then blow dry them it makes the feet very soft and therefore ten times more tickle sensitive as well," the van driver said, sounding out-rightly sadistic. "What we're a gonna do here is give you three helpins of slopping and a swilling your feet with the cream we put on it already Chuck ol' Chuckles and we'll dry em' up real nice for you too...three times."

As the van driver spoke Chuck's eyes rolled in his head in disbelief behind his blindfold and a look of total terror had come into Daisy's eyes.

"Oh please, don't tickle him no more," Daisy pleaded. "Especially iffen his feets are all soft and sensitive like..."

The van driver chuckled meanly and then Sam and Victor

turned off their portable hair dryers. Chris and Adam quickly went to work slathering the groom to be's bare feet with a second coating of skin cream.

"Wow, his feet feel softer already..." Adam commented handling Chuck's left foot with a tight grip as he liberally lotioned it.

A short while later the sounds of Chuck's laughter filled the cabin as all six men, each of them armed with a stiff quill-like feather tickle tortured the young man's heated, sensitized feet...

"HAH, HAH, HAH, oh glory be!" Chuck screamed. "They was right Daisy, they was right, oh tarnation! They was right! After creaming up a guys feet and a blow-dryin' them it sure as fucks does make them all the more ticklish...OHHHHHHHRRRRRR HAHAHA!"

The six men all glided the tips of their feathers up and down and up and down the bottoms, sides, arches and heels of Chuck's quivering feet. Daisy watched transfixed as her fiancé's feet sweated skin cream as the six men all feather tickled them... Once again she wanted to be lick tickling her man's bare feet...

After they had all tickled Chuck's creamy and heated feet for nearly forty five minutes Adam was busily stroking the groom to be's erect cock, his piss slit aimed at the jar of his already accumulated sperm.

"OHHHHHHHHHH, wh-when this over I'll sure have lots to think about you varmints," Chuck prattled and his huge muscles flexed involuntarily in the tight bondage. "Never knew that my danged cock could get so worked up just from a bein' tickle tortured like all of you a been doin' to me here..."

It took a while longer this time but once more Chuck shot a hefty sized load of spunk, adding substantially to what was already in the jar.

"OHHHRRRRRR, fucking fucks fucker, whoever you are, milkin' and exploitin' my danged manhood here…" Chuck panted as he seemed to cum and cum once again.

When he was done he once more drawled, "I gots to pee…" sounding very Forrest Gump again. Adam quickly picked up another jar, said, "Go for it Chuck" and while Adam held his deflating cock in hand Chuck pissed a long frothy yellow stream into the jar… The sound of his pissing as it filled the jar was somehow erotic to the tied down groom to be…

"Bet that's a relief eh Chuck ol' Chuckles?" the van driver asked.

As he finished pissing Chuck smiled behind his blindfold and said, "It sure is…STEVE…"

The van driver's jaw dropped and he said, "WHAT? How in hell did you know?"

That said the driver whipped Chuck's blindfold off him. Chuck looked up at his older brother and his smile spread longer on his bearded and handsome face.

"Who else calls me Chuck ol' Chuckles?" Chuck asked and looked around at the rest of the assembled men, smiling more-so. "I see your gang's all here…"

"At what point did you know Bro?" Steve asked as he began untying his younger brother's feet while Jack untied Daisy.

"I thinks it was when you had my socked feet in that danged shoe shiner machine…" Chuck responded. "Somehow I just knew…or maybe I knew all along. I means, you're the one who told me about that secluded spot at the lake where a couple could go to be alone and I knows how Jack just loves playing mean jokes on guys…although I never would have knowed it was him the way he kept on with that yuk, yuk, yuk and yum crap."

All the guys and Daisy laughed...

Once Chuck was fully untied he climbed down off the table...

"Dang it all, this was some way to initiate a groom you fuckers," Chuck laughed.

He quickly put on his shorts, tee shirt and socks...

"Tarnation, you boys left my danged sneakers at the picnic area where you all snagged me and Daisy here," Chuck said.

"It's not a problem," Steve said. "I'll drive you straight home so you don't have to go a walkin' around in your socked feet."

"Thanks man, and this time I'll ride up front and untied, iffen that's okay with you big brother," Chuck said with a grin and wiggled his toes under his socks.

"Its fine with me and for being such a good sport about all this and not being pissed off with us I'll even buy you a new pair of sneakers..." Steve said and gave Chuck's shoulder a squeeze.

"Yeah, and to show you that my heart is in the right place me and Chris will come over to your house on the wedding day to help you climb into your monkey suit, er, your tuxedo, Adam said.

"No tricks though Mister Video..." Chuck said, pointing a wagging finger at Adam.

"I'll bring you your tuxedo socks," Chris said with a grin.

"Somehow I knew you would you crazy sock fetishist you..." Chuck said with a grin.

"Well, I'm a glad Chuck isn't pissed off over all this, but I don't know that I can say the same for me…" Daisy piped up, holding the jar filled with her fiancé's collected sperm.

"Aw come on Daisy, it was all in fun after all," Chuck said, hooking a huge arm around his bride to be…

A short while later Chuck and Daisy were in the back of Steve's van as he drove them and the rest of his buddies' home… Chuck sat with his arm around Daisy. Next to him in a bag were the jar of his sperm, the jar of his piss and the sheer socks he had worn…

Chuck and Daisy's Wedding Day...

"HAW, HAW, HAW!" was the sound that emanated loud and piercingly from Chuck's living room after his two buddies Chris and Adam had arrived to help him get into his tuxedo.

Perhaps it should be said that they had arrived under the pretense of helping the groom to be into his tuxedo. After all a guy always needs a hand doing his bowtie, his cummerbund and just to make sure his patent leather shoes are properly spit shined. It should also be said that tickle torturing a groom on the day of his wedding is a shitty thing to do to him. But Chris and Adam knew that Chuck had at least two and a half hours before he had to be at the church and they could not think of a better way for the doomed groom to spend his last couple of hours as a free man...

At the sound of the doorbell Chuck dashed to the door, wearing just a pair of white boxer shorts and knee high (OTC) black sheer thick and thin socks, the socks having been given to him a couple of days earlier by Chris, the sleaziest sock fetishist of them all as he had come to be called.

"Yeah, who is it?" Chuck called out irritably. "I'm a real busy boy here today, getting a ready for my weddin' and such!"

"It's us you big doomed groom," Adam called out jovially.

"Well you boys are sure here early," Chuck said as he threw the door open and admitted his two buddies. "I'm a just loungin' around here; I ain't even ready yet to get into my danged monkey suit..."

"Lookin' good chuck," Chris said as he glanced down at the groom to be's sheer socked feet. "And may I say that those sheer socks look awesome on you..."

"Awesome, shmawesome," Chuck said with a wide grin. "Cain't believe I let you talk me into wearin' these here femmy looking danged socks..."

"Well, it is a tradition after all Chuck," Adam said. "It's an old rule of etiquette..."

"What old rule of etiquette?" Chuck asked as he and his two buddies stepped into the living room.

"In old fashioned times it was decreed that the groom wear sheer silk socks with his tuxedo on his wedding day while his best man and groomsman all wear solid black socks," Adam explained.

"Sort of like the bride when she wears something old and something new, something borrowed and something blue," Chris added.

"Oh fuck me you guys, I cain't believe we's a here talkin' about my danged footwear and such," Chuck laughed. "Almost reminds me o' how you and the rest of those guys tickle tortured me a few days ago...I still get a chills when I a think about that..."

"Hmmm, so what you're saying is that you enjoyed that eh Chuck?" Chris asked.

"Well, I wouldn't exactly say enjoyed now..." Chuck said.

"Say, where's that jar of your juices?" Adam piped up. "I do hope that you gave it a place of honor somewhere..."

"I keeps it on a shelf in the extra bedroom," Chuck replied, sounding real sleazy. "Got it rights there alongside those other smelly socks you fuckers put on me when you slipped my danged feet into that thar shoe shiny device you a tickled me with."

Chris and Adam looked at each other, grinned, and Adam asked Chuck, "Can we see?"

"I suppose so," Chuck replied, foolishly turned his back on his two buddies and started heading toward the door to the living room, padding on his socked feet. "Although for the life of me I cain't imagine why you all want to look at a jar that contains a guy's most precious fluids..."

As Chuck was about to exit the living room Chris and Adam dashed quickly up behind him, grabbed his muscular arms and before the groom to be could react they whirled him around and back into the living room.

"H-hey, what are you mugs up to a now?" Chuck complained as his socked feet almost left the floor, his two buddies practically hoisting him.

"Got the rope Adam?" Chris asked.

"I sure do Chris," Adam laughed in reply as they held the struggling groom real tight. "Got the electric toothbrush?"

"I sure do Adam," Chris also laughed in reply. "As Jack would say, yuk, yuk, yuk, and yum..."

"Say, what are you two mugs up to here?" Chuck panted as his hands were quickly and efficiently tied behind him. "I gots to get married today...I don'ts have the time for any tomfoolery and such..."

"You have more than two hours before you have to be at the church to get hitched, locked, stock and barrel to Daisy Chuck ol' boy..." Chris said as he took an electric toothbrush from his pants pocket.

Chris clicked the toothbrush on to the highest setting, making the bristles spin and whir and what looked to Chuck like a hundred miles per hour...

"AW no, no, you scoundrels, you villains, you wouldn't tickle a guy on his wedding day now would ya?" Chuck barked in sheer terror as Chris approached him with the buzzing electric toothbrush and from behind him Adam slid Chuck's boxer shorts off him.

"Say Chuck, you wouldn't happen to have some aloe cream around here would you?" Adam asked, grabbing a handful of one of Chuck's ass cheeks after having gotten his boxer shorts off him.

Chuck's cock stuck out long, hard, beefy and thickly veined in front of him...his balls hanging down real low and succulent looking...

"A-aloe cream?" Chuck drawled. "What in tarnation do you wants with aloe cream?"

"Better yet, I'll just use some of that sperm that I collected from you to lube up your shit chute…" Adam laughed and dashed out of the room in search of the jar filled with Chuck's goop.

"WHAT IN THE FUCKING FUCKS are you mugs up to here?" Chuck ranted at Chris as he held up the whirring and buzzing electric toothbrush.

"We're gonna make sure you know how to dance at your wedding today Chuck…" Chris said and Chuck's jaw dropped in total horror.

A short while later the sounds of Chuck's insane laughter filled the living room as he hopped and danced around on his sheer socked feet.

"HAW, HAW, HAW!" the burly groom to be guffawed crazily, Chris' electric toothbrush wedged deep in his cum slicked asshole and buzzing madly. "OH GAWDS, what a shitty thing to do to a poor sap on his weddin' day, of all days! HAHAHA! OH TARNATION and fuck me, those bristly bristles are a makin' me nuts here!"

Sitting on the couch Chris and Adam watched as Chuck hunched his shoulders up, his huge biceps muscles flexing involuntarily as he danced and stomped around. The groom to be laughed his head off all the while trying to force the invasive device out of his being tickle tormented hole…

"Think we should start helping him get his tuxedo on?" Adam asked Chris.

"Nah, we still have plenty of time before he has to be at the church…" Chris replied sadistically. "Let's let the guy dance his tickle troubles away…"

THE PREQUEL AND SEQUEL TO THE EROTIC VIDEO

"SIGNS OF A STRUGGLE"

Starring: Rich and the Southern accented "Strong Man"
Created by: the guys at Struggling Artist Media and added onto and
written by Author: Christopher Trevor

"Here we are Rich, a nice new hotel room just for the two of us," the nameless southern bodybuilder said in a fiendishly jolly sounding tone of voice as he quickly opened the door to the new room he and his prize would occupy. "I know you're goin' to like this room, its real classy lookin' bud..."

Over one of the bodybuilder's huge and broad shoulders handsome and muscular Rich was being lugged like a sack of dirty laundry, his hands securely bound behind him at the wrists and his feet tied as well, at the ankles.

"mmmffff..." Rich murmured a bit incoherently behind the

"black silk gag", the center of it tied into a thick ball and wedged good and tight in the poor guy's mouth, the black silk gag being one of the bodybuilder's favorites it seemed when silencing his prize.

As the extremely strong man quickly locked the door of the hotel room, thus quickly shutting out the world's eyes, not wanting anyone to see him with his captured prize Rich squirmed in his draped over position, balanced on the man's shoulder. The handsome and muscular captured young man was clad in nothing more than a pair of his silk and very sexy looking tight fitting beige colored boxer briefs (direct from an "International Male catalogue") and a pair of black thick and thin sheer dress socks, OTC style, just for the record. Rich being scantily clad, bound up and gagged was the very obvious reason why the bodybuilder needed to enter his hotel room unseen. Granted, getting the door opened with Rich slung over his shoulder was not the easiest of tasks, but the time spent at the gym had really paid off for the Southern sounding strong man where this venture was concerned...

"I think this room will do very nicely for us to continue our game," the strong man said jovially, running his hand lovingly down Rich's muscular back as it dangled in front of him. "Hope you like it as much as I do bud..."

Rich summoned all the strength he could and arched himself upwards on the man's shoulder. The sinewy muscles in his stalwart and ripped back and over-sized biceps flexed involuntarily with his efforts. He chewed angrily on the gag tied in his mouth and his eyes took in the sight of the new hotel room, the third hotel room in a row where he would be forced to play this deranged man's "Game of Bondage" as his captor had come to call it.

"RRRMMMFFF...remmeee ro!" Rich blubbered; trying to say let me go, as he squirmed in his miserable tied up and gagged position. "FRUCKING chird rotel roon rou rawt nee roo..."

"Good boy Rich, very good boy indeed, you know how to count, this *is* undeniably *the* third hotel room I've brought you to," the man laughed, grabbed Rich's arm and lowered his prize back down to a dangling position over his shoulder. "You woke up quick this time huh bud?"

Rich simply nodded his head in reply against the strong man's crotch as he was carried toward the bed...

"Looks like next time I'll have to dose you a bit more powerful huh?" the man asked Rich, sounding very Southern now as he unloaded him, plopping him down on the bed.

"RRRMMFFFF!" Rich grunted looking up at the man with pure unadulterated anger showing in his beautiful chestnut shaped brown eyes.

"Aw yeah, I love carryin' you around Rich, you really are quite the handsome package I must say, but I also love putting you down, you're no light-weight after all..." the man chuckled. "All that muscle sure does test my strength and weigh after a while..."

"Rhi Ranna rho own," Rich garbled, trying to say I want to go home, but the strong man simply leered at him and nodded his head "no."

Rich pulled himself into a seated position on the bed, digging his socked feet into the soft and plush covers as the man who had captured him days ago looked him over, he looked him over lustfully and somewhat psychotically... Rich tried to ignore the fact that the man was looking hungrily at the erection he was sporting in his tight fitting beige boxer briefs... A fear hard erection that was what Rich had come to call it. No way was he turned on by all this madness that he had been so unwittingly thrust into.

"Man oh man, I really like those underwear's you got on Rich," the nameless man said with a maniacal looking grin on his face. "I really am so, *so* glad that you decided to wear those the day I, how should I say this, the day I decided to acquire you for my game. Now, I need to go out to the car to get the rest of our stuff, meaning my bondage equipment and your extra socks, ha, ha... So you know what that means buddy..."

"GRRRFFFF!" Rich reeled, pissed off not at just this heinous game of wits that he had been unwittingly thrust into, but also pissed over the fact that for three whole days all this man had allowed him to wear were his sexy underpants and his socks.   Granted, the man had changed Rich's socks for him a few times during the "bondage game", citing how he wanted him to be tidy, but not once had he changed Rich's underwear. Granted again, at the outset of the game, when Rich thought this was all on the up and up and just for some challenging fun the man had allowed Rich to wear other articles of clothing. But for the last two hotel rooms he had been brought to it had been his sexy tight fitting boxer briefs and black sheer dress socks and sometimes his thick white sweat socks...

"I'll have to tie you so you don't think about running off on me until I'm ready to start the game again in real earnest," the man said, rubbing his chin and seeming to mull over his options. "This is after all an in between for our game, as you know. If you were to leave in between our game that just wouldn't be fair now would it? No, not fair at all and I do want you to win this game fair and square Rich. It wouldn't be fair for my side of the game if you were to get loose while we weren't playing. Now, how should I leave you tied while I go out to the car and get the rest of our stuff?"

"Rever Nind dat," Rich prattled behind his gag, trying to say never mind that. "Rust ret nee no!"

"Just let you go?" the man asked, sounding astounded. "Just let you go? But Rich, after all the trouble I went through in getting us a new hotel room? I mean, just look at this place, total class! Now that is not what I call proper appreciation bud..."

"RRRMMMFFF…" Rich said, tears nearly filling his eyes.

"I know what it is, I know exactly what it is buddy, you're still ticked off because I made you ride in the trunk of my car, that's it, isn't?" the strong man asked and reached into his deep pocket and brought out a long length of semi thick rope.

In response Rich again nodded "yes."

"I know that was rather not nice of me Rich, but how else was I supposed to keep you hidden from any cops or troopers that might have happened along the road?" the man chuckled. "I mean, having a tied up and gagged guy in the passenger seat might have made them suspicious. And I doubt they would have understood our game…"

"RHIS Ris rot a dame," Rich said, trying to say this is not a game. "ROU Ridnatted nee…"

"You say I kidnapped you, I say it's a game, either way you look at it we're having a great time Rich…" the man said sadistically as he approached his prize with the rope. "Now, hold still while I get you secured to the bed and then I'll go and get our stuff from the car…"

A few moments later Rich was lying on his back on the bed…

The nameless man had tied a goodly amount of the rope tightly around the erect plump bulge in Rich's boxer briefs and then meanly stretched the slack of the rope between Rich's muscular legs before finally tying the end of it off to a slat under the middle of the bed… When the man had stretched the rope real taut Rich reeled in a mixture of pain and ecstasy behind his silk gag…

"Now remember what I told you Rich, no struggling for the moment or trying to get untied, this *isn't* part of the game" the man said, squatting next to the bed and squeezing and twisting one of Rich's very pronounced nipples as he taunted him. "If you move the wrong way you're liable to get your most prized possession yanked clear off you buddy…"

Rich dribbled pre cum from his tied up cock in his boxer briefs and simply stared up at the ceiling as he chewed angrily on his gag… His cock was betraying him again, making his captor think he was somehow enjoying this twisted game of bondage and wits. But truth be known, whenever Rich's nipples were squeezed or twisted he always dribbled pre cum from his wide sexy cock slit, as he called it…

"You just lay there and relax and I'll be right back before you know it buddy," the man said laughingly, let go of Rich's nipple and dashed out of the hotel room, closing and locking the door behind him.

"mmmfff…" Rich moaned miserably, his tied up cock feeling a mixture of pain and ecstasy as he thought back to how this had all begun three days ago….

Three days, poor Rich, personal trainer at a gym called "Leo's Iron Man Gym" thought, three whole days since he had stupidly and unwittingly agreed to this nameless client's challenge, three whole days since "the game" as it had started out being called had begun. As he lay there tied in such a heinous position he wondered why he had agreed to the game to begin with. He chewed his black silk gag and knew the answer instantly, he didn't need three guesses to figure it out, it was because it was a challenge and in all his life Rich had never turned down a challenge. His well muscled body was evidence of how the handsome young man challenged even himself on a daily basis. When the man had mentioned how he had supposedly endured the same challenge, and at the hands of a female Rich could not help but say "Yes" when the same exact challenge was presented to him. Three whole days since he was held prisoner in the first hotel room, although at that time the princely handsome young man didn't know he was a prisoner, at least not yet; at that time he simply thought he was being tested in his wits, strength and endurance, and being tested in one of the most challenging ways at that. It was not until the man dosed him (that's what the man called it Rich called it drugging him although the man assured Rich that it was totally harmless) and brought him to the second hotel room that the robust and handsome trainer knew that he had a definite problem, the problem being that the Southern sounding body builder (the strong man as Rich had come to call him) was not planning on letting him go. Okay, Rich thought, the strong man did say that if; *if* he got himself untied he would be free to go. He even said he would drive Rich home, hardy har, har. (Rich knew that to be driven home would be yet another LONG, long ride in the trunk of the strong man's car. And Rich knew that they had done hours upon hours of driving at this point. The poor guy knew that he was nowhere near what he called home.) But with the way that he tied him each time, the mounds of knotted rope, the double and triple knots he applied, the very confining and intricate positions he was put in (the hogtie being the worst, although the strong man taunted Rich of how that seemed to be his favorite position, it was the one he tied him in the most) made it just about impossible for the poor guy to get himself untied. Even all his muscle strength was not enough it seemed for him to break free of the binding and knotted ropes...And now, *now* he was tied up in a third goddamned hotel room and he knew that was how he would stay until this deranged man either tired of him (which was not likely whatsoever) or he himself finally managed to get himself untied and the man would let him go and even drive him home...hopefully...*hopefully...*

As he lay there tied at the cock and balls of all things on the bed in the latest hotel room he had been brought to Rich stared up at the ceiling, chewed more-so on his gag and the handsome trainer's mind wandered back three days...

"There you go Sir, that's the exact motion you want to achieve with each rep you do," Rich said as he squatted behind the Southern sounding muscleman as he sat on a weight bench hoisting two dumbbells as he worked his very huge, very broad shoulders.

As has been mentioned Rich is a personal gym trainer. He

is employed in a gym called "Leo's Iron Man Gym." The trainer is approximately thirty years old, he stands just a tad shy of six feet tall, has brown short cut hair and deep chestnut shaped brown eyes. His body is well toned from not only being a trainer at the gym that employs him but also from being one of their most dedicated members. His legs are muscular and they are shaped and thick veined like two tree trunks, especially around the calves. His stomach region is washboard flat and hard from the hundreds of sit-ups he punishes himself through on a weekly basis. His chest is robust and strong and adorned with two pencil eraser-sized nipples, what some of the women he has dated call his "Man Sized Tits." His arms are long and lankily muscular, his biceps round and nearly the size of bowling balls with triceps that are sinewy and bulging...

Rich's hands stayed positioned just under the Southern sounding man's elbows as he lifted the dumbbells slowly up and then down, working his shoulders real hard. (Looking back on it now Rich figured that the man would have to keep those shoulders strong if he wanted to carry his prize the way he did.) Looking handsomer than a prince Rich was clad in the uniform of the gym that he worked for, black gym shorts with white stripes down the sides, a white tank top with the gym logo stenciled on the front of it and Rich's nametag pinned to the side, black sneakers and thick white sweat socks tucked down into his sneakers. It had been three days ago that the owner of the gym, Leo himself, had asked Rich to train the Southern sounding strong man, citing the reason for the request being that Rich had no scheduled clients at the moment and that Rafael, the trainer who usually worked with this client had mysteriously not shown up for work the last two days. Rich agreed and Leo personally brought the handsome as a prince Rich over to his client.

"Sir, this is Rich, he'll be working with you for today and possibly tomorrow as well," Leo said to the Southern sounding well built man.

The Southern man shook hands with Rich, a strong and

powerful handshake Rich duly noted and said that it was a pleasure to be working with him. Rich smiled his killer smile, the one that always melted the ladies hearts (and perhaps some men's as well he figured, being in this business it could not hurt to be a tad seductive) and agreed with the Southern man that it would be a pleasure working with him as well. As he shook hands with him Rich had to wonder why such a robust and well-built guy such as this needed a personal trainer. The guy actually looked like he could be a trainer himself, little did poor Rich know at that moment. The guy's shoulders were as wide as a doorway. His hands looked big enough to punch holes through walls with. His arms were hugely muscular. So why in hell did he need a trainer? But Rich was not one to shirk his responsibility, nor was he one to shirk the opportunity for some high paying commissions. As Leo left the two men alone Rich quickly realized that he had not been told the client's name. Well, that was not a problem he thought, seeing as all he would be doing was training him through some workout routines...what poor Rich didn't know yet was that the tables would soon be turned and he would be the one being trained...

As the man lowered his muscular and powerful looking arms for the final rep Rich allowed his client's elbows to land in his open hands. Then the man slowly lowered his arms the rest of the way and set the dumbbells down with a slight thud.

"Very good Sir, that was three superb sets for your shoulders," Rich said and quickly gave the man's shoulders an intense squeeze and flexing massage. "Do some stretches for your shoulders and then meet me at the triceps machine."

"Good deal Rich," the man said jovially in his Southern sounding accent.

As the man stretched as he had been instructed Rich walked over to the triceps machine and set the weight for his client, not aware of the way his client was drinking in the sight of him and plotting...

It was about ten minutes later when the Southern sounding strong man returned to the hotel room. Rich watched as he walked in, quickly locked the door behind him and set his medium-sized luggage down on the writing table. Grinning meanly the man made a big production of opening the luggage and allowing his prize to see the contents within. Rich's eyes opened as wide as saucers at the sight of all the white rope and the extra pairs of his own socks...

"MMMFFFFF Rod, ro," Rich murmured into his gag, trying to say, God no.

"Okay Rich, time to try a new position now," the man chuckled as he grabbed a good amount of rope from the luggage. "You can keep your wedding socks on for now, how's that feel?"

Rich nodded "no", feeling absolutely miserable as the man approached him with rope...

His cock oozed more pre cum...

The man chuckled at the sight of that...

While the man stood perfectly balanced in front of the triceps machine Rich stood behind him watching his form as he performed the exercise, only three days ago in the captured trainer's mind...

"Very good Sir, good fluid and steady motion," Rich said, his hands just scant inches from the man's burning triceps.

"Thanks Rich, that's a real compliment coming from a studious trainer such as you," the man commented, turning his head slightly to smile at Rich.

"Head straight Sir," Rich said, playing the part better than well of the concerned trainer. "Always keep your head straight and your eyes focused when using this machine. And thank you for the compliment, that's very nice of you to say..."

Rich watched the man's motion as he worked through the last two reps of his set...

"And...rest," Rich said as the man allowed the weights to settle at his feet and he let go of the weight bar in front of him. "Very good, two more sets like that and then I'll raise the weight on this machine by twenty pounds... I'm sure you'll be able to handle that."

"We'll see Rich, one never knows what one can or cannot handle," the strong man said and gave Rich a gentle pat on the arm in between stretching. "Although for myself, I'm always up for a challenge. What about you Rich? How do you feel about challenges?"

"Well Sir, it depends on what the challenge is I would have to say," Rich said and pointed at the triceps machine. "Time for your next set Sir..."

"What if I said I had a challenge in mind for a guy just like you Rich?" the man asked the trainer as he gripped the weight bar again. "A guy *exactly like you*... What would you say to that?"

"Well, I would of course say that that sounds very interesting Sir," Rich said, looking quizzically at his new client. "What exactly did you have in mind if I may ask?"

As the strong man now said, "There you go Rich, tied up just like the first time I tied you," Rich wished how he had NEVER accepted the man's strange and totally bizarre proposal. The poor trainer now found himself in a hogtied position, his hands still securely bound behind him with the slack of the rope extended down to his socked feet as he squirmed on the bed. His biceps curls were wrapped and secured in rope as well and pulling his muscular arms back, making it that much more difficult to propel himself around on the bed. He did however thank God that the man had untied his poor cock and balls.

"Remember the first position I tied you in bud?" the man asked Rich, reveling in the sight of his prize as he squirmed miserably on the bed, trying in vain to get his twitching and trembling fingers around the knots in the hogtie, but with all the double and triple knotting the man had done, it was virtually impossible it seemed. "Three days now that I tied you in your jeans, your white tee shirt and your white sweat socks, that's the only difference bud, that this time in this position you're in your sexy underwear's and wedding socks…"

Rich turned his head and the rest of his body and looked at the man in total uninhibited anger.

"RRRMMFFFFFF!" Rich panted behind his now red bandanna style gag, it tied snugly over and in his mouth as he struggled.

The red bandanna gag was also a throw-back to the first time the man had tied him. Rich thought miserably how if the man was going to replay his bondage positions in the order that they first started then his next position would involve armpit tickling, his armpits being tickled, he dreaded. And poor Rich's armpits were the most ticklish part of his well-toned body, as the strong man had found out…

"Just get yourself untied Rich and you'll be on your way home faster than you can say lickety, dickety, split," the man laughed meanly and aimed his video camera at his captured prize. "And of course I don't need to remind you that if you don't get untied we'll just move onto the next position…"

"RRRMMMFFFFF!" Rich snarled at the man, spittle flying from the sides of his gagged mouth.

"The challenge that I have in mind for you Rich is not one that many men or women enter into that quickly," the Southern sounding man said as he hefted the triceps bar up and down, working his muscles the way Rich had instructed him to, Rich remembering again, as he struggled how all this had began. "Your buddy, that other trainer, Rafael, he entered into my challenge and he did rather well at it…if I do say so myself that is… But again, the challenge I am describing to you is one that you should think over before agreeing to it…"

"If Rafael did well at it then why isn't he here to train you Sir?" Rich asked, standing next to his client and speaking softly now, thinking that he was entering into a way to make some extra bucks without Leo or the other trainers knowing it.

"Rafael is not here to train me, I suppose, because he needed some time to rest up Rich," the man said with a grin on his face. "As I said, what I'm proposing is very challenging indeed. I mean, Rafael is okay, he's not hurt. It just took a lot out of him…"

Rich pursed his lips together as the man finished his set and set down the weights and let go of the weight bar. Rich knew that he was much stronger than Rafael, much stronger indeed, and if *he* had done well at the man's challenge then Rich figured it should be a walk in the park for him. Also, his macho pride was not about to allow Rafael to have one upped him in the eyes of this mysterious client.

"Thinking about it Rich?" the man asked his prey as he stretched.

"Maybe, maybe not…" Rich replied his eyes darting back and forth as he spoke. "Like I said it all depends on what you have in mind for me…"

The man's cock tingled because he knew that he had snared yet another pigeon for his coop…

"Tell you what Rich, this really isn't the place to talk, too many ears if you know what I mean," the man said, sounding conspiratorial. "Lets get me finished up here and then we'll go and get a bite for lunch. We'll talk privately…and if you agree to my challenge we'll drive to your place to pick up some extra socks for you…"

"Extra socks?" Rich asked, his eyebrows raised and a stupid looking smile playing on his handsomer than handsome face…

"And maybe an extra pair of underwear's as well okay?" the

man asked and smiled at the dumbfounded Rich.

Extra underpants and socks Rich thought, as he struggled fiercely on the bed, determined to get himself untied this time. (Actually each time he was newly tied he was determined to get untied, but each time proved impossible to the poor guy.) Extra goddamned socks so he could stay tidy the man had said, jeez, and he had fallen for that. The man chose the socks from Rich's night table drawer himself, a couple of pairs of thick white's and a pair or two of black thick and thins OTC style to be exact, what the man mockingly called "Wedding Socks." And fuck it all the tied up trainer thought as his trembling fingers found a knot and then miserably lost it seconds later, they really were supposed to have been his damned wedding socks of all things. He struggled some more, grunting and gasping behind his gag... If Linda, his now Ex-fiancée could see him at this moment. Wedding socks indeed, because he recalled how she had gone with him to the tuxedo fitting when they were still engaged and how she and the sales guy there had convinced him to purchase the sheer socks, citing how a proper groom always wears sheer silk socks on his wedding day. Rich could not have given a fuck what kind of socks he wore when getting married, all he knew was that as the wedding day loomed closer he had gotten cold feet, and the sheers would not have been enough to keep him warm. So he kept the sheer socks and backed out of the wedding, much to Linda's chagrin and anger. She told him she never wanted to see him again...

"RRMMFFFFFF..." Rich grunted and managed to get his fingers around his tied up "wedding socked" ankles, gripping them real tight while still facing forward in the awful hogtie and trying to maneuver his fingers to the knots without seeing them.

"There you go Rich, you're getting there buddy, *you're getting there now...*" the man said enthusiastically as he filmed his unwilling star.

But then, Rich could not maintain the position he was in and his fingers slid off his ankles...

"GGGRRRRMMMFFF!" he railed in anger, his fingers twitching and flipping. "GRRRFFFF! Grod an it!"

"AWW, poor Rich, but you know you really shouldn't be taking the lord's name in vain by saying things like God damn it bud, it really isn't nice, not at all," the man chuckled and Rich's mind wandered back again to the day he had met this strange sounding and yet very interesting man.

"Order whatever you like Rich, its on me," the man said as they now sat in a restaurant that was near the gym, after the man's workout was complete and he had showered and dressed.

Leo had given Rich the rest of the day off, seeing as he had no other clients scheduled.

"Thanks, that's really nice of you I must say," Rich said, crossing his sneaker foot on his knee.

Rich was now clad in his jeans, white tee shirt and sneakers with thick white sweat socks.

"So tell me, now that my curiosity is peaked off the Richter scale," Rich said, looking at the menu as he spoke. "What exactly is this challenge that you're trying to get me to agree to?"

The man smiled and said, "Let's order first" as a fine-looking waiter approached their table...

They ordered a healthy and hearty salad each and as the blond waiter walked away the man said, "Bondage Games."

"Bondage games?" Rich repeated, only making it a question now. "Is that what you said Sir? Bondage games?"

"You heard me correctly Rich, don't be so naïve about it now," the man said, sounding even more Southern at that point for some reason. "Many, many people participate in bondage games nowadays. For them its part of the sexual arena, but not for me Rich, not for me."

Rich simply stared in awe at the man as he spoke and the trainer could not deny that he was starting to sport a stiffy in his jeans.

"So uh, if it's not in the sexual arena for you, then why do you want to play bondage games?" Rich asked grabbing his white sweat socked ankle as it rested on his knee, him looking intently across at his host. "And more precisely, why do you want *me* to play bondage games with you?"

Rich was reluctant to admit that for some strange reason he was very, very intrigued by the challenge that this man had just presented to him.

"Well, you working as a trainer in a gym and with the exercises you forced me through, it shows me that you're a person who's a real contender," the man said, him also looking intently across the table. "You strike me as someone who really enjoys a challenge."

Rich rubbed his hand under his chin and grinned at the Southern sounding man who had no name...

"You're kidding me right?" Rich asked, chuckling a bit as he said it. "Did one of my buddies at the gym put you up to this or maybe my ex fiancée?"

"No one put me up to it Rich, it's just my way of having some very unusual and very interesting fun," the man said, sounding very sure of himself.

"And uh, you've had other people agree to this game, as you call it," Rich said.

"Sure have," the man replied. "Both men and women alike enjoy these games Rich, that I can assure you of. On a psychological level it also helps participants to relinquish control of things for a while and let someone else do the driving for a bit…if you would…"

Rich sat silently for a few moments before speaking again. While he was silent the man took in the beautiful sight of him and knew he had chosen well once again where this venture of his was concerned. While Rich mulled their salads were served and they dug in, both men very hungry from their respective workouts earlier at the gym.

"Okay, let's say I agree to this," Rich piped up after swallowing a mouthful of salad. "What do I have to do?"

"Nothing really, except get yourself untied after I tie you…" the man explained. "I mean, for the most-part I'll be the one doing all the work…"

"Get myself untied?" Rich asked as he slowly brought a forkful of salad to his mouth. "Um, how did Rafael do getting himself untied?"

"Well, I'm not going to lie to you Rich but it took your buddy five positions before he was able to free himself," the man said with a smile.

"F-five positions? What the hell does that mean?" Rich asked.

"It means, that after a good amount of time tied in one position I untied him and then re-tied him in other positions, to see how he would fare…" the Southern sounding man said. "It's not good to leave a person tied in one position for too long, both for physical and psychological reasons…"

"And he agreed to be re-tied after you had untied him?" Rich inquired a look of amazement on his face.

"He sure did, he agreed to the rules after all…" the man said and ate a forkful of his salad.

Rich could not believe that once Rafael was loose that he would let himself be tied up again, and in another position no less.

"It must have been frustrating for him huh?" Rich asked.

"A bit, you see, I did tease him some of the time while he struggled," the man chuckled. "If he could have gotten untied the game was over and he was free to go, if not, well, then it's another bondage position."

"And he's okay now?" Rich went on.

"Like I told you back at the gym it took a lot out of him but yeah, Rafael is fine," the man said. "Struggling in bondage can get to a guy…or a woman after a while…"

Rich put his fork down and leaned back in his chair, his long shapely legs stretched out in front of him. The man glanced down admiringly at Rich's feet…

"You've tied up women too?" Rich asked.

"Not yet Rich, but I am hopeful," the man said and winked, looking lecherous. "I did have a woman tie me up though, now that was an experience to remember let me tell you bud…"

Rich took a deep breath and looked at his host, a feeling of uncertainty coursing through him, but his curiosity most definitely peaked…

"You, uh, said that if I agreed we would have to stop by at my place for extra socks and underwear's," Rich said. "Why's that?"

"Well come on now Rich, all guys need extra socks and underwear," the man said and chuckled heartily. "You do want to be tidy after all..."

As the man filled his mouth and swallowed Rich said, "Okay, I'll do it Sir." And as the man chewed, looking down at his plate he gave Rich a thumb-up sign...

Now, as Rich recalled that fateful moment the man was busy tying the poor trainer in a new position. Rich had squirmed and rolled around on the bed in his hogtied position for a good forty-five minutes before the man teasingly told him that it was time for another new position, or more precisely the second of the first positions that the man had tied him in...

Rich nearly cried as the man dosed him and then went to work preparing his subject for the next bondage position, firstly, by preparing him by taking his black sheer "wedding" socks off him along with his sexy beige boxer briefs underwear's as the man called both those skimpy articles of Rich's clothing... And if history repeated itself in this new hotel room then Rich knew that the next bondage position would entail his poor armpits being tickle tortured...

A short time later Rich found himself clad in just his white boxer shorts and his white sweat socks, (the bottoms of them a tad dirty, that being sexy somehow to the man who was his captor.) As he had stripped him the first time the man said the same thing this time as he unclothed his prize, "I want to make you a bit more comfortable Rich."

"RO, ro, ron't rie nee agin..." Rich prattled, trying to say "No, no, don't tie me again," still gagged with the red bandanna as the man positioned him atop the queen sized bed and prepared him for the next squirming and struggling session. Rich then found himself tied in a crucifixion position, his muscular arms stretched out real taut and his wrists tied off to the ends of the bed board, his white sweat socked feet pushed together and roped off to a slat under the bed, and just to be doubly cruel the man had lashed Rich's knees together as well, thus not really giving the poor guy a chance at even getting his feet freed.

"Now, like I told you the first time I tied you like this a couple of days ago, I suggest you get loose this time, because just like last time I'm going after your pits again," the man said, sounding totally lecherous.

"RHO RO!" Rich ranted behind his gag, trying to say "Oh no!" "Riss rot rood roo rickle a ragged uy!"

"It's not good to tickle a gagged guy?" the man asked as he raised his fingers as he walked toward the bound and gagged Rich. "Well, being that what it is then, all you need to do to avoid the upcoming laughter is to get free Rich; it's as simple as that...so simple..."

So simple Rich thought, or at least three days ago he thought that. Three days ago when after he and the man had finished their lunch the man had driven both of them back to Rich's apartment to get the necessary items that the man had mentioned. In Rich's apartment, or more precisely, in Rich's bedroom he and the man sifted through Rich's most private of drawers, namely his underwear and sock drawer...

"Okay, I'll use this toiletry satchel to put these in," Rich said, reaching into his sock drawer and taking out a couple of pairs of thick white sweat socks.

"Now, now Rich, you need to be more creative than that," the Southern sounding man said, taking the white sweat socks from Rich and tossing them back in the drawer.

"More creative? It's just socks Sir, and underpants," Rich said, wondering why he had agreed to this peculiar game.

"Well, yes, it's just socks, I grant you that, but still, this is an adventure you're going on in a way, wouldn't you agree bud?" the man asked and reached into Rich's sock drawer.

"I-I suppose so," Rich said and nearly blanched when the man held up two pairs of black sheer thick and thin OTC dress socks. "Now, these are real pretty Rich, plus you're already wearing white sweat socks."

"Okay, okay, those are fine I suppose," Rich said impatiently, visions of Linda fleeting through his mind and the day she had made him buy the silk socks when they were still planning on being married.

"Something wrong Rich?" the man asked as Rich deposited his socks into the small satchel along with the beige underpants.

"No, no, I'm fine Sir, just fine," Rich said. "Just these dressy socks remind me of someone, but I'm fine..."

The man smiled and to make Rich feel better he reached into the trainer's sock drawer and took out one pair of thick white sweat socks. Rich smiled dumbly, said "Thanks Sir" and deposited the white sweat socks in the satchel as well...

"I was, I uh, I was going to be married you see but as the day loomed closer and closer I guess you could say I got cold feet and backed out," Rich said, sounding a bit regretful. "And when my ex fiancée and I had gone for my tuxedo fitting those two pairs of socks you just chose for me, well, she and a sales guy at the tuxedo store had chosen them for me. They're actually called "Wedding Socks. I didn't return them when I called up to cancel the tuxedo order..."

The man smiled and said, "Well, they might just bring you some luck after all Rich. You might just wind up winning this "Bondage Game" after the first position because of those "Wedding Socks" of yours...

Rich let himself be led by the arm out of his apartment as the man grinned...

"RHHHAAAAAAAAAAA!" Rich now squealed in loud peals of shrill and tormented laughter as the man straddled him on the bed and dug his fingertips deep, deeper and deeper yet into the trainer's armpits, squiggling them around in there as he went. RHOOOOOOOO!"

"Ah, the sound of manslaughter, I mean man's laughter, sorry Rich," the man chuckled.

"REAVE NY RITS ARONE!" Rich ranted his head up off the bed, trying to say "Leave my pits alone."

"Now Rich, you know the deal here, you get untied and I'll gladly leave your moist and smelly pits alone, it's as simple as that," the man said mockingly and twirled his fingers in Rich's armpits some more.

"RHRRRHAHAHHHAHAHAHHHHAAAAAAA!" was all Rich could say.

"Maybe at some point if you still don't get untied I'll have to shave these pits for you buddy," the man laughed, tugging on the hairs in Rich's deep armpits. "You know, I don't know about you Rich, but tickling a guy's armpits is real fun for me. How about you bud?"

Rich squealed his response in uncontrollable throes of laughter as the man was relentless in tickling him and tickling him...

"Yes, I can see you enjoy it too bud," the strong man said mockingly.

"RHO, RHO, RHY ont!" Rich prattled and spitted, trying to say, "No, no, I don't!"

"Get untied Rich, that's all you have to do..." the man repeated.

Rich's eyes filled with tears as he laughed and laughed and laughed, just as he had done the first time he was tied in this crucifixion position.

"RHY RON'T WAN ny arnits raved..." Rich panted, the gag stifling the words, "I don't want my armpits shaved..."

"Well, from the position you're in it really isn't about what you want is it Rich?" the man asked and tickled his treasure still more. "I think after all our time together it's more about what I want...true bud?"

Without answering Rich's mind then wandered to the past again...

"What are we doing at a hotel Sir?" Rich asked as the man pulled his car up in front of the place.

"Why not a hotel?" the man asked in reply.

"Well, I thought you would want to play your game at your place," Rich said.

In response the man laughed real heartily and stepped out of his car. Rich shrugged and followed his host.

Say uh, Sir, can I ask you something that's been on my mind?" Rich called out, dashing around the side of the car, holding his satchel in hand.

"Sure thing Rich, what is it?" the man asked as he took his luggage of bondage equipment from the trunk of his car.

"What's your name?" Rich asked as they walked into the hotel lobby and up to the front desk.

"Isn't this just one of the most beautiful hotels you've ever seen Rich? We're going to have a GREAT time here," the man said, seeming to ignore Rich's question where his name was concerned and gestured toward the book on the hotel clerk's desk. "Sign us in if you would bud..."

That said Rich's face took on a look of incredulousness as the man walked toward the elevator bank...

"Sir?" the desk clerk called out to Rich. "We accept American Express and Visa and Master Card as well..."

"Uh, yeah, sure," Rich said softly, not believing that he was going to pay to be tied up.

Rich took care of the transaction and then joined his unnamed host on the elevator.

"What the hell was that all about?" Rich asked as the elevator ascended.

"What was what all about Rich?" the man asked him in response.

"You made me pay for our room..." Rich said.

"I didn't MAKE you do anything bud," the man laughed. "You did it on your own. You're still not tied Rich."

"And what does that mean?" Rich wondered aloud.

"It means buddy, that you're still free to walk out of here on your own power," the Southern man said jovially. "It's only once you're tied that the game will have officially begun. So, if you want to back out and get a refund for the room as well, go right ahead..."

That said the man pointed at the bank of buttons on the wall of the elevator…

"Nah, fuck it, we're here now," Rich said softly and held up his satchel of socks and underwear. "I'm up for your challenge Sir. Trust me; we won't be here all that long…I'm sure I'll get out of your bondage knots real quick and we'll be on our way…"

The elevator stopped, the door opened and the two men proceeded to what would be the first room where Rich would spend hours upon hours tied up and gagged…

After the man stopped tickling Rich's armpits for nearly an hour or more the trainer was too winded to stop the guy from re-positioning, re-tying and re-socking and re-dressing him yet again. Rich found himself tied and dressed in the same fashion as he had been the first time he was tied this way, two days ago in that first and blasted hotel room….

Rich took in the fact that he was again miserably tied in a hogtie, the difference from the first one though being that the length of rope extended from his bound wrists to his bound feet was much shorter this time, making it that much more difficult for the guy to try and get free. It also left him with just about no mobility whatsoever. The man had also tied a long length of rope around and around Rich's muscular upper torso and tied the slack of it around and around his big round biceps, once again twisting the guy's arms back. This of course Rich realized was to make it even more difficult for him to get free. It was at that moment that the trainer started to become concerned for his safety…

"RHEY, riss ris ot reashy," Rich sputtered, now gagged with a mouth filling ball-gag and trying to say, "Hey, this is not easy."

"Of course it's not easy Rich," the man chuckled. "If I made it easy it wouldn't be a challenge now would it? And you do so love a challenge I know, you did say so yourself after all…"

The man drank in the sight of the now bare-chested Rich, his lower body clad in tight fitting black spandex pants with red stripes down the sides and a pair of his black sheer wedding socks

"Ah gotta say Rich, that it was a delight to find those spandex numbers of yours under your jeans the first time I stripped you back in the first hotel room…" the man said, aimed his camera at the bed and filmed his prize as he struggled anew.

"RHO lad rhoo ike rhem," Rich said, trying to say, "So glad you like them…"

"Those "wedding socks" of yours sure do work well with them too I gotta say bud," the strong man said and reached around from his filming point to tweak Rich's socked toes.

"RHEMMEEE RHO!" Rich prattled, desperately trying to say "Let me go!"

"Nah, not yet bud, I still have lots of video tapes I can fill up," the Southern sounding man laughed and his cock tingled as he watched Rich squirm atop the bed, trying desperately to reach the knots in the hogtie he was in. "And besides all that, you know the rules of the game bud…all you gotta do is…"

"RHY RO! RET unried…" Rich said behind his gag, trying to say, "I know, get untied."

"You got it Rich; you got it down pat bud…" the man said sounding totally wicked. "You really are quite the intellect I must say…"

To try to stave off the feelings of helplessness Rich's mind wandered once again back to the first hotel room, back to the first bondage position, back to when he had agreed to this insanity as he had now come to call it…three days his mind wandered back yet again…

"Nice room you, or should I say, I, got us..." Rich said as he took in the surroundings of the comfortable looking room, although he knew he was not there to be comfortable.

"Oh come on Rich, I'll make it up to you, I know that was a mean joke to play on you, but I will make it up to you..." the man said as he set his luggage on a writing table.

Standing against a wall with his arms folded Rich asked, "Yeah, how?"

"Well, lets see now, you said you would be untied in no time right?" the man asked with a wide smile.

"True," Rich agreed.

"Well, as soon as you're untied I'll treat you out to a real expensive dinner, from soup to nuts," the strong man said and opened his luggage. "We'll even have desert. How does that sound? How do you feel?"

"It uh, it sounds fair, I suppose," Rich said, taking in the sight of the mounds of rope that filled the man's luggage and the various lengths of different colored cloth that he would undoubtedly be gagged with.

A look of trepidation came over the handsome trainer's face...

"Changing your mind Rich?" the man asked as he extracted two lengths of rope from the luggage.

"Uh, no, so, uh, what do I do now?" Rich asked with a nervous looking grin.

"Now you just let me go to work bud, just let me go to work..." the man said sounding real dapper now as he stood before Rich with the two lengths of rope. "Hands behind you, feet together if you would..."

Rich swallowed hard, turned and faced the wall and crossed his wrists behind his back...

The man went to work quickly and efficiently winding rope around and around Rich's wrists, knotting it as he went and then winding it more before knotting it again...

Rich took deep breaths as the man squatted behind him and did the same with his sneaker clad feet...

"You okay so far Rich?" the man asked. "How do you feel bud?"

"I, uh, I feel okay, I guess, just can't believe that I'm really being tied up, and so tight at that..." Rich said.

"Well, it is going to be a challenge," the man said and got to his feet behind the handsome trainer after he was done lashing his feet real tight.

"Okay, now I'll put you on the bed and complete the tie..." the man said and with no effort whatsoever it seemed lifted Rich off the floor and into his huge muscular arms in the position of groom carrying his new bride over the threshold.

"WHOA, you sure as hell are strong Sir," Rich laughed as his tied feet left the floor. "But what did you mean about finishing the tie? My hands and feet are tied and..."

"I mean, I need to finish the hogtie Rich," the man said. "And actually this will be the first hogtie I ever did...I'm a novice at it..."

Holding Rich real tight by the bed the man looked into his captive's eyes and laughed. The laugh sounded a bit insane to Rich and the lifted and tied guy had to wonder just how much of what the Southern sounding guy was saying was true... Would this actually be the first hogtie he ever did? He did say that he had tied up Rafael after all? Hadn't he tied Rafael in a hogtie Rich wondered.

Then, Rich found himself dropped on the bed and hogtied, his hands extended back behind him and tied off to his already tied feet...

The man chuckled as he filled Rich's mouth with the balled up silk black gag... If the personal trainer didn't know better he would swear that the balled up black silk gag was actually a pair of OTC nylon dress socks tied together. What was it with this guy when it came to bondage and socks?

"Okay Rich, you can get started any time you want on getting free," the strong man said jovially. "And just for prosperity I think I'll film some of this... You don't mind do you bud?"

"RRRMMFFF, frim rit?" Rich asked, lying on his side as he tried to say, "Film it?"

"Sure bud that way we'll both have something great to look back on in time..." the Southern sounding man said and headed for the hotel room door.

"RHEY, RHERE are ROU roin?" Rich asked, trying to say, "Hey, where are you going?"

"Oh, just out to the car to get my video camera," the man replied. "Now you keep on working there Rich. Who knows, you might be untied before I get back and then we're off to dinner..."

Rich looked at the man in disbelief...

"But then again, maybe not huh bud?" the man laughed and walked out of the hotel room.

"ROH ROD," Rich murmured, wondering just what the fuck he had agreed to here.

As Rich thought about how he had struggled the first time the man tied him his mind wandered back to the present and how he now again found himself in a tie that was reminiscent actually of the second hotel room he and the nameless man had frequented... It had been awful Rich recalled, how he thought the man had decided to let him go, seeing as he couldn't get untied from any of the ties he had found himself in. Rich figured that the guy would cut him some slack, no pun intended. Instead the poor trainer found himself struggling some more...after he had been kidnapped that is...

"Hmm, you don't seem to be doing as well as Rafael did Rich," the strong man said after the trainer had been tied in his spandex pants and "Wedding Socks." "Maybe this game isn't for you after all..."

"Well, I'm sure if you gave me more time maybe I would do better at it Sir," Rich said. "But it kills that I didn't earn that dinner you mentioned..."

"Oh well, you don't need to worry about that Rich," the Southern sounding man chuckled. "I'll give you more chances to get untied down the line..."

Then the man laughed his insane sounding laugh and Rich found himself "dosed" for the first time...

Terror filled the handsome personal trainer as for the next few days he found himself to be stored in the trunk of the strong man's car. He drove for miles upon miles it seemed to the now captive Rich. He fed Rich while he sat up in the trunk of the car on deserted roads; poor Rich blindfolded now as he sat tied up in the trunk. He pleaded with the man to let him go, saying how the game had turned out *not* to be a game after all... The strong man reminded Rich over and over of what he had agreed to, how all he would have to do is get untied when they had resumed the game and he would then be free to go. Dismay filled Rich's heart each time the man finished feeding him, packed him back into the confines of the trunk, gagged him and drove again for hours and hours of miles... When the need to relieve himself was at the breaking point the man kept his captive blindfolded and his hands bound behind him while Rich stood and urinated in the bushes on the deserted roads they were driving on. Rich was not gay but somehow, as the guy handled his cock, holding it steady as he pissed the handsome personal trainer found himself laying what his ex-fiancée used to call a hard woody. This got the man chuckling meanly and twice he took the brazen liberty of jacking Rich off twice in the bushes... The times while on the road when Rich had to do a bit more than piss was the most humiliating for the young man. The strong man untied Rich's hands but kept one of Rich's arms bent up against his back and his wrist of that arm tied off to a rope that was tethered around the trainer's colossal chest. With his one hand free Rich was made to squat blindfolded on the road and do his business. He thanked God that the man had brought along toilet paper...

It was at the end of the second day of driving when they had arrived at the second hotel where Rich would be made to continue the man's "Bondage Games..."

Now as he struggled, squirmed and rolled around maddeningly on the bed in the third hotel room, clad in his spandex pants and black sheer "Wedding Socks" Rich's eyes once more filled with terror when he saw the Southern sounding strong man shut off his video camera and prepare to dose him...

"Rhy wront ray ror ris rotel roon," Rich said behind his gag as he sat up in the trunk of the car upon him and the Southern sounding man's arrival at the second hotel as he tried to say "I won't pay for this hotel room..."

The man had parked his car on the road not too far from the hotel but far enough away so that no one would see his prize in the trunk while they talked.

"No, it sure looks like I will be paying for our accommodations from here on out Rich," the man said and ruffled his captive's hair. "Got to make sure no one sees you bud...And I'll be paying in cash from here on out, can't risk any credit card trails you know..."

The man laughed meanly, shoved Rich back in the trunk and drove his car up to the main entrance of the hotel...

Now, back once more in the present time Rich found himself newly hogtied, wearing just his sexy beige cotton boxer briefs with the black waistband on them along with his sheer thick and thin "Wedding Socks" ala Linda and that damned sales guy at the tuxedo store. Rich 's hands were tied at the wrists behind him, the slack of the rope extended down to his feet in a criss-cross fashion and then tied off around and around his socked ankles. The poor guy's forearms were tied off just under his elbows by a few lengths of tightly knotted rope as well, thus making it that much more difficult for him to reach for the knots in the hogtie behind him. His legs were tied at the knees as well by a short length of rope, keeping his legs meshed together as he struggled fruitlessly. His captor had used the duct tape gag on him for the second time. If Rich had had to choose which gag he detested the most since having agreed to all this madness he would most definitely have said the duct tape. It felt awfully sticky and totally imposing as it pressed meanly against his lips. As he struggled once more in the bondage he grunted angrily and looked up at his captor as he filmed him... He filmed him... Rich could not believe at the outset of all this that he would be filmed while in the bondage throes... But filmed he was and filmed he was being. He had no idea how many tapes the man had already filled with what now seemed like hours upon long hours of endless struggling to get untied. When the man had returned to their first hotel room with his video camera and began filming his struggling captive Rich was incredulous.

"RHEY, rurn rhat rhind roff," Rich had squabbled behind his gag when the filming had begun, as he was actually trying to say, "Hey, turn that thing off!"

"Now Rich, we may need these tapes later on, just in case you don't get free right away, as you said you could bud…" the strong man said as he inched around his captive, filming him.

"RHAT roes rhat nean?" Rich prattled, trying to say "What does that mean?"

"Just that you may want to watch some tapes of yourself as you try to get untied, just to see what you did wrong if you couldn't get untied…" the man laughed behind his camera. "I hope that makes sense to you bud, it works well enough for me…"

Throughout all their conversations as they prepared for this venture the man had never once mentioned filming the trainer while he struggled in the bondage…and just for the record, no, it did not work well for the captured personal trainer…

As Rich managed to arch his body forward he also managed to move his fingers with a great effort to reach for one of the knots in the hogtie at his "Wedding Socked" feet.

"There you go Rich, I think this time you just might do it bud," the Southern sounding man said, trying to build up Rich's confidence as he snagged a knot in his trembling fingers.

Rich then managed to move his tied up feet a tad forward and besides the rope around them he felt the soft silky material of his "Wedding Socks." The thoughts that went through his mind at that moment of how when he had first chucked those damned socks in his sock drawer he figured he would never wear them, once he had left Linda that is. And now he was wearing them, and in a situation that he never would have conceived being in, in a million years. Instead of wedlock his "Wedding Socks" had come to personify a different type of security device altogether at the moment…

"Ronna reht rhout riss rine," Rich moaned through the now soggy duct tape gag as his finger curled around the knot in his socked feet.

"You're gonna get out this time Rich?" the strong man asked, sounding totally sadistic. "I sure do hope so for your sake. You've spent more time tied up than anyone else that I've ever done this to bud. And in my case it'll sure save me money, seeing as I won't have to pay for anymore hotel rooms..."

Rich looked over at the man in disbelief at the comical statement he'd just made. It was ridiculous. The man didn't need to spend any money on hotel rooms. All he had to do was let Rich go... that was it...as he kept saying to his captive...it was that simple...

But then, awful frustration set in hot and heavy all over again as Rich lost his slight finger grip on the knot near his socked feet...

"RRRRRRHHHHHHHHHHHH!" the captive trainer screeched through his duct tape gag. "RRRRHOOOOOOO rho, rho, rho..."

Tears filled the young man's eyes as the strong man stepped over to the bed and whisked the duct tape gag off his captive.

"Aw man, I was so close that time," Rich muttered. "I got to get my hands back there again and..."

But as Rich spoke the Southern sounding man said, "Quiet now Rich," and replaced Rich's duct tape gag with the red bandanna one.

"RRRHHHMMMFFFFF!" Rich bellowed angrily. "Rhod, rish roo roudn't rag nee..."

"You wish I wouldn't gag you bud?" Rich's captor asked jovially, quickly retrieved his video camera and resumed filming his bound up handsome captive. "Well, I'll tell you bud, the visuals of you struggling while all tied up in your underwear and socks is very appealing to the eyes for viewers. The added sounds of you grunting behind a gag of any kind are a bonus of auditory appeal.

"Vrewers? RHAT VREWERS?" Rich gasped and managed to lift his upper torso.

It was at that moment that the captured personal trainer realized that he was starring in a video that would more than likely find its way to underground porn shops. He struggled now not with just the thoughts of getting out of this predicament, but also with a determination to get his hands on all the videos his captor had taken of him. Rich had seen videos in the X-rated stores akin to the one he was now starring in. But those videos had been staged and shot in a production studio. This one would look like it had been staged and shot in a production studio...but unfortunately for the unwitting star it was all too real.

"MMMFFFFF! REMME RHO!" Rich bawled, trying to say "Let me go" as he struggled in the unforgiving hogtie.

He arched his muscular body back and managed to turn himself on his side. His captor smiled ecstatically behind his video camera as Rich involuntarily flexed his huge pecs, bounced them a few times and gave the camera a breathtaking view of his huge hairless chest as he struggled.

"Oh man, thanks Rich, that was a great shot," the Southern sounding man commented. "Although I don't see how being on your side will help your cause."

The man laughed and Rich looked at him in utter aggravation.

"RHEMME ROUTA REHERE, REEESE!" Rich pleaded, sounding almost pitiful as he tried to say, "Let me out of here, please!"

"Looks to me like I'm wearing you down again bud, just like in the second hotel room I had you in," Rich's captor said, now sounding totally sadistic.

Still lying on his side, chewing on the bandanna gag and struggling in the knotted ropes Rich nodded affirmatively.

"Yep, running out of steam bud, that's what happening to you," the strong man laughed. "By the way, did I mention that the knots I made in that hogtie you're in get tighter as you struggle?"

In response to the man's last question all Rich could say was, "RHHHOOOO ROD, RHOOO!", trying to actually say, "Oh God, No!"

The man simply chuckled meanly and Rich struggled himself back onto his stomach.

"Okay man, seeing as you can't seem to get out of that tie either I say its time to try something else," the strong man said.

Rich was dismayed as the man began undoing the hogtie to prepare him for the splayed out position on his stomach that he knew was coming next. If it was to be just a reenactment of how he had been tied in the second hotel room Rich knew full well what was coming then... As he was dosed into a dreamlike state Rich's mind wandered. He thought of the feel of those silk socks on his feet, how they stretched all the way up to just below his knees, and how his ex fiancée and a prissy tuxedo sales guy had duped him into buying the sheer numbers. He wondered somehow if all of this was his payback for having left Linda... As the strong man readied his captive for the next bondage position Rich found his mind wandering again to the past...but this time not to the past when he wound up as the Southern sounding man's bondage captive, but to a night months before his wedding to Linda was to take place... It was a night when Linda had accompanied him for his tuxedo fitting...

Rich was standing on a raised platform wearing the pants of the black Armani tuxedo he had decided to rent for the occasion of the wedding and a white tee shirt. His jacket, tuxedo shirt and bowtie were all hung on a nearby hanger.

"Okay Sir, stand straight and look directly into the full length mirror in front of you," the prissy salesman said as he handled the bottoms of Rich's pants, folding them upwards so that they were the proper lengths for alterations purposes.

Glancing down Rich rolled his eyes in disbelief as the sales guy's long blond hair hung in his face. He looked at Linda as she looked at him adoringly.

"That tux is going to look great on you Rich, please be patient," Linda said. "I know all of this isn't really for you...being that you're a personal trainer at a gym and all...I know that suits and formal wear really isn't the attire that a trainer is into..."

"Oh, is that what you do for a living Sir?" the sales guy asked, his hands roaming upwards under Rich's tuxedo pants. "You're a personal trainer at a gym?"

If Rich didn't know better he could have sworn that the guy was toying with his damned black ankle length sweat socks, leftovers from his workday with clients at the gym.

"Yeah, I work at Leo's Iron Man gym," Rich said to the guy, winking at Linda as he said it, trying to scare up more business for himself, obviously.

"Well that sounds impressive," the salesman said, looking up at Rich, two of his fingers most definitely tucked down in one of his sweat socks now. "Um, tell me Sir, being that you work in a gym do you always wear sweat socks like these?"

"Most times yeah," Rich replied, glancing down as the guy handled his sock of all things.

"Well, you can't wear these for the day of your wedding Sir," the salesman said reproachfully.

"Well of course not," Rich said, sounding as if the guy thought he was a dumb muscle head. "I plan to buy some black nylon dress socks and..."

"We sell socks here Sir and ones that are "Wedding Appropriate" if you would..." the sales guy said, cutting Rich off in mid sentence.

"Wedding appropriate?" Rich asked. "And what does that mean?"

"Well Sir, as the groom you should be wearing silk sheer socks with your tuxedo while your best man and groomsmen all wear solid black nylon socks," the sales guy explained. "It's an old fashioned form of etiquette. It's really not adhered to much nowadays but if you want to have an old fashioned and traditional look for your wedding you might want to opt for the "Wedding Appropriate" socks."

"Oh Rich, it's the same as the bride wearing something old and something new, something borrowed and something blue," Linda gushed as the salesman snapped the elastic in one of Rich's black sweat socks.

Rich looked at Linda and then down at the sales guy...

"Okay, anything you say bud, but please, if you don't mind, just make the alterations on my tux trousers and stop playing with my damned socks huh?" Rich asked the guy.

The guy chuckled and then later Rich found himself leaving the tuxedo store with Linda and carrying a bag which contained two pairs, not one, but two pairs of the sheer thick and thin black OTC socks...the socks he would not be wearing for a wedding, but rather for his time spent as a non-willing bondage participant in a twisted game of wits, strength and endurance...

As Rich's mind cleared and climbed back up to the present it was the feel of the strong man's hands on one of his sheer socked calves and his toes that first brought him around...

"RHHHO ro, rot rhis aren..." Rich sputtered through the black silk gag that was again tied over his mouth, the knot set in the center of it filling his craw. "RHIS RHIS a RAWFUR rosishon..."

"It's an awful position bud?" the Southern sounding man asked him and chuckled.

Rich was now lying on the bed on his stomach, his sexy muscular legs spread out real wide, his hands tied behind him and his feet tied off at the ankles, the rope around his ankles stretched down to the legs of the bed and tied to them, keeping his legs real taut and pulled tight. Rich curled his fingers back in search of knots in the ropes around his wrists but utter dismay engulfed him when he realized that his captor had done it to him yet again. All the knots in the ropes binding his wrists had been tucked underneath where his fingers could not get to. How his captor ever expected him to get free that way was beyond him. Once again he was gagged with the black silk gag, the ball of it crammed in his craw. At this point Rich was more than convinced that the black silk gag was an old pair of black nylon OTC socks tied together and re-fashioned into a gag. As Rich chewed the gag involuntarily he wondered whose socks they had been...

"It's really a better position for squirming Rich," the man said and this time instead of filming his captive straightway he was snapping pictures of him with a digital camera. "As opposed to the hogtie that is..."

As the man loomed over him and snapped a picture of his handsome gagged face Rich contorted himself sideways and railed, "RUT RHY RANT REASSSHH RHE ROTES..." as he tried to say, "But I can't reach the ropes!"

"RRRMMMFFFF!" Rich squawked as the man snapped and

snapped his picture.

"Aw, such a handsome and boyish looking guy you are Rich," the strong man said. "You know, I was thinking that after this I would simply let you go...seeing as you're just not having any luck whatsoever with this challenge you've agreed to..."

Rich lay back down, faced his captor and nodded his head "yes, yes, yes," squeaking out the words, "Rhemme Rho," trying to say "Let me go."

"But then I came across another hotel in my catalogue where we could go bud," the Southern sounding man said happily. "It says in the catalogue that they have four poster beds in this hotel I found..."

Rich angrily shook his head no as his eyes filled with tears...

"Aw Come on Rich, give it some thought bud," the man laughed and snapped more pictures from Rich's angle at his sheer socked feet. "With a four poster bed I would be able to tie you real nice in a spread eagle position and with you that way I could finally shave those hairy and bushy pits of yours. What do you think?"

Rich rolled his eyes in his head and struggled fruitlessly...

"Okay, I'll let you lay there and think about it buddy," the strong man chuckled. "While you do that you can try to get free I suppose...but if you don't I'll just retie you in another position..."

"RRRMMMFFFFF..." Rich squabbled and lifted his upper body upwards, his toes curling back under his sheer socks.

As he struggled and tried in earnest to get his fingers under the ropes around his wrists to reach the knots he thought of how awful he had felt a day or so ago when the strong man had brought him into the second hotel room they would occupy. For his captor's benefit they had been issued a room on the ground floor of a hotel which had separate small villas, rather than one big building housing the hotel. In the villa they had been issued they would be the only occupants, as the desk clerk had explained to the Southern sounding gentleman that this was actually the hotel's off season and they didn't get many guests at this time of year. The strong man said that that would be ideal for him, seeing as he was working on a very special and important project. As the desk clerk handed the man his room key he asked if he had any luggage or cargo with him. Smiling as he left the main lobby the strong man said, "Oh yes, I have some very precious cargo in the trunk of my car…"

The man drove his car to the villa and parked directly in front of the room that he and his unwilling star would occupy. Before carrying Rich into the room the strong man set up his video camera, aiming it at the door to the room. A few moments later a befuddled and angry Rich was carried bound up and gagged into the hotel room by the strong man. He carried his captive in the manner of a groom carrying his new bride over the threshold… As Rich was lugged into the hotel room he thought miserably of how this was how he would have been carrying Linda…had he married her that is.

The "bondage games" began again as they had in the first hotel room as they continued relentlessly in the third hotel room…

As Rich now struggled fruitlessly atop the third bed he was tied to the poor trapped guy wondered miserably how he would fare when they had arrived at the fourth hotel and when he would be lashed to the four poster bed… It was obvious to the young man that whoever the Southern sounding strong man was he did not intend to release Rich anytime soon…

"Ready for the next position Rich?" the strong man called out…breaking the personal trainer's concentration.

Rich fussed and grunted behind his gag as the strong man untied his feet and peeled his sheer socks off him, rolling Rich's white sweat socks with the dirty bottoms on them back onto his captive's feet...

"There you go buddy, I know how much you prefer your white sweat socks as opposed to the wedding numbers..." the man chuckled and gave Rich's feet a squeeze as he raised them upwards toward Rich's bound hands, once more hogtying him...

As night descended and as the man was once more changing Rich's gag the sound of a desperate personal trainer was heard saying, "Let me out, come on already, let me out..." as he struggled and was then gagged, "MMMFFFFF..."

ABOUT THE AUTHOR

Christopher Trevor was born in July 1963 and grew up in New York City. As soon as he was old enough to know how he began writing fiction and has been writing gay erotic/fetish stories for the past ten to twelve years at this point. He became an avid reader as well from the time he knew how and reads everything from fiction, to non-fiction to biographies of interesting and unusual people, people who have made a difference or who have paved the way for others. Christopher attributes his writing artistic inspiration to artists such as Etienne, Tom of Finland, Tagame, The Hun, and most notably Joe T, who Christopher has had the pleasure of speaking with and even meeting over the last few years. Christopher states, "Joe T encouraged me to write about my fetish because I was embarrassed about it at the time. Joe T said that when we are embarrassed about something that makes it even more enticing somehow." Christopher totally agreed and never stopped writing in this genre. Erotic writers who inspired Christopher Trevor were: Tom Shaw (author of "That Day at the Quarry), C.S. White (author of Big Sur), Larry Townsend (author of countless erotic novels), and Mason Powell (author of the classic story "The Brig.")

Christopher discovered that not only did he enjoy writing erotic tales but that after his first bondage experience he had a genuine flair for it. Writing to erotic oriented magazines about his first bondage experience truly opened the floodgates for Christopher where this style of writing is concerned. Christopher thanks the handsome and muscular "Greg" for that experience way back in time. Christopher took "Creative Writing" courses every semester during his high school years and while other friends of his stopped writing what they loved to write about as time went on Christopher never let a day go by when he didn't write something... "I feel that if I don't write every day I will die," Christopher has said many times over.

Foot fetish stories and all things related; spanking fetish, erotic shaving, muscle bondage, tickle torture, and hardcore stories are just a few of the areas of gay eroticism that Christopher enjoys writing about and inspiring in others as well. As one internet buddy said to Christopher where the black socks fetish is concerned, "Until I started talking with you I never gave a thought to my socks when I got dressed for work in the morning. Now when I pull my dress socks on every morning I get a chill up my spine."

Christopher is proud of the erotic effect he has on people...

Christopher Trevor is also the author of:

The Executive Guide to Foot Fetishism and Office Discipline

    1-887895-36-1

Executive Ties That Bind

    1-887895-37-X

Don't! Stop! That Tickles!

    1-887895-31-0

The Taming of Dominick

    1-887895-45-0

Timmy and The Hong Kong Tailor

    1-887895-30-2

Love, Torture and Redemption

    1-887895-32-9

Timmys Ticklish Trials

    978-1-887895-74-3

The Gym Instructor

    978-1-887895-44-6

Milked

    978-1-887895-66-8

Erotic Street Blues

    978-1-887895-97-2

The Abusive Wager

    978-1-887895-04-0

Terry's Appointment and Other Tickling Stories

    978-1-934625-08-8

The Military File

    978-1-934625-21-7

Quirks

    978-1-934625-24-8

Timmy and the Evil Dr. Vonvellicator

    978-1-934625-42-2

Blackmail

> 978-1-934625-47-7

Tickled Kink

> 978-1-934625-49-1

Humiliation

> 978-1-934625-58-3

Discipline

> 978-1-934625-07-1

Revenge

> 978-1-934625-60-6

Taking Liberties

> 978-1-934625-65-1

Look for them where you bought this book, Amazon.com or
TheNazcaPlainsCorp.com

www.ingramcontent.com/pod-product-compliance
Lightning Source LLC
Chambersburg PA
CBHW071219260626
47162CB00004B/1360